THE L

SERIES TITLES

The Three Devils and Other Stories
William Luvaas

The Correct Response
Manfred Gabriel

Welcome Back to the World: A Novella & Stories
Rob Davidson

Greyhound Cowboy and Other Stories
Ken Post

Close Call
Kim Suhr

The Waterman
Gary Schanbacher

Signs of the Imminent Apocalypse and Other Stories
Heidi Bell

What We Might Become
Sara Reish Desmond

The Silver State Stories
Michael Darcher

An Instinct for Movement
Michael Mattes

The Machine We Trust
Tim Conrad

Gridlock
Brett Biebel

Salt Folk
Ryan Habermeyer

The Commission of Inquiry
Patrick Nevins

Maximum Speed
Kevin Clouther

Reach Her in This Light
Jane Curtis

The Spirit in My Shoes
John Michael Cummings

The Effects of Urban Renewal on Mid-Century America and Other Crime Stories
Jeff Esterholm

What Makes You Think You're Supposed to Feel Better
Jody Hobbs Hesler

Fugitive Daydreams
Leah McCormack

Hoist House: A Novella & Stories
Jenny Robertson

Finding the Bones: Stories & A Novella
Nikki Kallio

Self-Defense
Corey Mertes

Where Are Your People From?
James B. De Monte

Sometimes Creek
Steve Fox

The Plagues
Joe Baumann

The Clayfields
Elise Gregory

Kind of Blue
Christopher Chambers

Evangelina Everyday
Dawn Burns

Township
Jamie Lyn Smith

Responsible Adults
Patricia Ann McNair

Great Escapes from Detroit
Joseph O'Malley

Nothing to Lose
Kim Suhr

The Appointed Hour
Susanne Davis

PRAISE FOR

THE THREE DEVILS AND OTHER STORIES

"Wildly imaginative and always engaging, Luvaas's stories delve deep into the sacred and profane of human existence, no matter the time and place, no matter how fantastic or ordinary. Surprising in their compassion, heartbreaking in their loss, and often terrifying in their grim mission to survive, Luvaas's characters reflect our own desire to find love, meaning, and community, even in the face of the collapse of all that we believe we most want, need, and cherish—a final test of what angels and demons define us when faced with our own annihilation."

—KIM BARNES
Pulitzer Prize Finalist
author of *In the Kingdom of Men*

"I've been shouting it for years, but now I'll shout it louder: William Luvaas, my friends, is a wild-eyed genius."

—LAUREN GROFF
National Book Award Finalist
author of *The Vaster Wilds* and *Florida*

"Luvaas ranges from the philosophical to the deeply personal, masterfully intertwining topics as wild as cults and climate doom and as subtle as self and family. A nightmarish vision of the inevitable conclusion of the world we've created today."

—CHASE DEARINGER
Chief Editor of *Emerald City*
author of *This New Dark*

Contents

"The apocalypse may be no fun to live through but in fiction it can offer thrills and chills—and insights into the human condition at the intersection of resilience and evil. William Luvaas delivers these and more. A Vietnam veteran at his wits'—and the world's—end. A professor who studies desperation and tries to save Picasso paintings. A woman who sees devils but might be a savior. Stalkers. The Night Crew. Truth Keepers. The Liberty Patrol. Dr. Doom. You'll meet them all. And, believe me, you'll be glad you did."

—MARK BRAZAITIS
author of *The Incurables*

"No American writer has as dark and vivid an imagination as William Luvaas, and his third collection of stories displays his gifts for mordant insight and wry prophesy at their ominous best. In the vein of Camus' *The Plague* and Saramago's *Blindness*, this modern-day Jeremiah paints a vision of a future in which the hapless and benighted struggle against epidemics of wrinkled air, mad crows, museum lootings, mountain survivalists and the roar of a vengeful planet. *Three Devils* is one of those masterpieces that is hilarious until it isn't—a window into the human psyche and the destiny of our species. A volume for the top of the discerning book lover's pre-apocalypse reading list. Don't wait until it's too late."

—JACOB M. APPEL
author of *Einstein's Beach House*

"That rare read, a post-apocalyptic odyssey that's fun. With humor, sparkling prose, sharp dialogue, and characters we can identify with, he explores a not-so-futuristic So-Cal world ravaged by foul-air syndrome, murderous cults, social collapse, and "Hunters" and "Scalpers" looting what's left. Like Cormac McCarthy with a sense of humor, Luvaas offers a fresh perspective on the existential disaster our species will face if it doesn't take drastic action now—yet the reader comes away from the book, incredibly, with a tiny hope that humanity is not lost while there are people left to observe it with such empathy and wit."

—GEORGE MICHELSEN FOY
author of *The Last Green Light*

THE THREE DEVILS

AND OTHER STORIES

WILLIAM LUVAAS

CORNERSTONE PRESS
UNIVERSITY OF WISCONSIN-STEVENS POINT

Cornerstone Press, Stevens Point, Wisconsin 54481

www.uwsp.edu/cornerstone

Printed in the United States of America by
Point Print and Design Studio, Stevens Point, Wisconsin

Library of Congress Control Number: 2024947475
ISBN: 978-1-960329-62-2

Cornerstone Press titles are produced in courses and internships offered by the Department of English at the University of Wisconsin–Stevens Point.

FOR CIN,

My most-valued supporter and creative soul mate.

ALSO BY WILLIAM LUVAAS:

Welcome to Saint Angel

Beneath the Coyote Hills

Ashes Rain Down

A Working Man's Apocrypha

Going Under

The Seductions of Natalie Bach

THE THREE DEVILS

At first no one paid it much mind. Some few claimed they saw it, but most didn't. The Woman On The Corner said she saw it whenever she stepped outside. "The air is all wrinkled," she said, "it looks like a shirt that needs ironing." Mr. Taylor, who lived next door, threw a hand at her and shook his head in disgust. "What color is this shirt?" he asked. They had never gotten along, even though they had lived side by side for twenty years. "She's a kook," he would tell you. The guy who parked his Caddy in his front yard, much to the dismay of Yolanda who lived across the street ("You'd think we live in a junkyard"), talked leisurely about it to people strolling by while he washed his car—sponging it down from a bucket of soapy water and buffing it with a chamois cloth three times a week. "Looks like a mirage you see hanging over the asphalt on a hot day, like heat waves." He had a Route 66 bumper sticker on the trunk of his Caddy, so you could assume he was familiar with the open road.

The Woman On The Corner nodded her head. "Like I been telling y'all: the air is wrinkled."

"I only saw it once," the Caddy lover noted.

But most in the neighborhood thought this was a lot of hooey, like people most everywhere did. Wrinkled air, for goodness sake. Mr. Hicks, who lived next door to Willy Jefferson, said if he'd learned anything selling insurance for thirty years he'd learned that people are more afraid than they need to be. "Now I'm not complaining. I wouldn't have a job if they weren't."

Willy nodded, but he'd always wondered why anyone would want to sell insurance. It seemed to him that insurance was an investment in disaster. Maybe we can't avoid it, but who wants to make a living off it? "I blame Facebook and Twitter and all that," he said. "Facebook has a billion users worldwide, most of them squawking horse shit."

Mr. Hicks had never known anyone who spoke as crudely as Willy did about serious matters. "That man could run for Congress if he cleaned up his speech," he told his wife. "He's smart enough. I often agree with what Willy has to say but never agree with how he says it."

"Politicians!" His wife frowned. "They're all alike."

True enough, many in the neighborhood—and all over the city—blamed politicians for the fuss, but couldn't understand how it served their reelection bids to spread alarm. Some blamed the media. Willy blamed them both and everyone else who was addicted to sensationalism. In truth, no one was to blame. Or everyone was. It was "something in the air," people said. Maybe you couldn't see it, but it was there—an invisible menace. The experts all agreed. Thomas Sanchez, on the corner of Edgehill, would thump the Bible he regularly read on his front porch and hold forth to passersby: "Doesn't surprise me any. It's all predicted in the Book of Revelations. There will be famine and plague and misery upon misery. Hungry wolves will prowl the streets—" glancing left and right as if anticipating their approach "—and snakes with blood-red eyes will crawl out from under rocks."

Macy O'Brien, who was one of the first Whites to move into the neighborhood ten years earlier, smiled politely. She taught literature at USC and had once taught "The Bible as Literature" but couldn't recall any passages about snakes with blood-red eyes. However, Thomas was broadly on the mark. The Good Book was full of fearmongering. She suspected many of its writers, especially the prophets, were paranoid schizophrenics. She would never have told Thomas this. He was a good man, and she wouldn't wish to offend him. Besides, if she carped with her neighbors about religion, she couldn't live in the neighborhood. It wasn't in her nature to carp with anyone. We are all just trying to get by, she knew. We all need some comfort in troubled times.

A little farther along she encountered Floria Hernandez who seemed quite agitated. "You know I din't believe none of that. I din't believe nothing. When is something you can't see and can't hear and can't smell, how you going to believe something like that? Not even a ghost or nothing. *El espectro*. Is invisible, right? So I no believe. But last night I see. I walk outside for taking out the garbage and think must be moon or something. But is no moon. Is a ball with spikes sticking out right on top my head, five feet on top. Then is gone." Clapping her hands, then gripping her arms and shivering. "Is bad sign, you think? *Un presagio*? Like flying saucer or something. You think?"

"A ball with spikes coming out?" Macy asked. She had seen an image like this somewhere. On the Internet perhaps. It made her uneasy.

This was the last time she saw Floria Hernandez on her afternoon walk. She asked other neighbors about her, but they just shrugged their shoulders. "Hiding inside maybe, like lots of other people."

Besides these three—The Woman On The Corner, The Caddy lover, and Floria Hernandez—no one else in the neighborhood had seen anything unusual, nothing paranormal, and most remained dubious; they even ridiculed their more impressionable neighbors. Thomas Sanchez might be placed in their company, but he didn't claim to have witnessed anything strange, merely bore witness that the Bible predicted strangeness and calamity. Calamity upon calamity. War upon war. Plague upon plague. So it didn't surprise him.

The difficulty with accepting what can't be seen, Macy thought, is that it has no boundaries, no limits, no definition. It could be anything. And nothing frightens us more than the unknown. We know death, for example. We may not see it coming, but from childhood we know it will come one day and know when it has arrived. We know when something is dead: glassy eyes staring blankly up in a fixed stare as if gazing into infinity. We can't see hope, but we know when it is thriving, observe it in people's eyes and in news headlines: *ECONOMISTS PREDICT AN UPTICK IN FALL QUARTER*. True, we can't see sickness approaching, the flu, for instance, but we are aware of its arrival: the scratchiness at back of the throat, the sudden sniffles and aching joints that predict misery. Whatever this thing was, it remained invisible, not just before arriving but after it had arrived. A chimera. This unseen was like all the others combined. A novelist in the city had begun a novel titled *The Great Unseen*, which was optioned by Netflix before he wrote a single word.

Some claimed they could see it or hear it, like chains quietly rattling or wind curling over the eaves of a roof. Some, like The Woman On The Corner, saw air wrinkle over houses or a transparent fog moving along the street. They were sincere and guileless. If this thing was an ailment, as some claimed it must be, then it was stealthier than the flu, creepier than Ebola. Suddenly just there, people said, seizing ahold of its victims. Some vanished from the face of the earth without a trace as if whipped away in an alien spacecraft. Mrs. Hernandez may have been one of these. It was widely reported that a woman in Vladivostok, Russia was walking hand-in-hand with her lover on the beach when suddenly his hand went limp and hers fell against her dress. He was gone. "The air ate him," she said, but this may have been a poor translation, although chilling. If the air could warp and distort and form a spiked ball over your head, if it could wash over surfaces in silent waves like surf washing up on a beach without a whisper and cling to them like sea water clings to sand, then why couldn't it gobble you up? Snatch you into the ether?

The minister down at the Pentecostal church on the corner of Jefferson promised parishioners that the Lord would redeem them when the appointed day arrived. Walking along the street, they would rise straight up like a rocket into the air. Or be dashed to the ground if they were nonbelievers, their bones splintering with loud cracks. Foul air, he promised them, couldn't enter God's house, but would invade the houses of the heathen. The pastor had never seemed more enthusiastic in his sermons, almost happy. But some in his flock wondered why the Lord would permit an invisible devil to beat him to the punch. If people were snatched up off the ground, why shouldn't they be snatched up in the rapture rather than by a demon? Eaten, some said.

While across town in an entirely different world, up north in West Hollywood (although tainted air was said to be present there, too), a spiritual leader named Baba Ram Baba assured his devotees that this "Foul Air business" was propaganda foisted on a naive population by "life-haters." Legs folded beneath him in a lotus position, rocking back and forth on his haunches, he resembled the Dalai Lama in his yellow robes. "It is a fog of ignorance like all things feared and desired by the unenlightened."

But this "Bad Air" or "Foul Air" theory was rapidly catching on. Some said it was just pollution which had plagued Los Angeles for years and most everywhere else, especially China. That March, for some reason, it had gotten particularly bad, which was odd since it was an unusually wet and windy month when you might expect pollution to disperse. Some crackpot posted a theory on social media that quickly went viral. He claimed the Foul Air was a neurotoxin akin to sarin gas that had been released by North Korea, which not only sickened people, but drove them mad. They twirled about in circles, pulling out their hair, becoming dizzy and winded. Some attacked their loved ones. It worked on both your limbic system and the frontal cortex, the seat of empathy and morality, causing people to do things they would not normally have done. More a mental than a physical ailment. Although, it was hard to understand why they would release a toxin that was spreading across the world on air currents and would eventually reach the North Koreans themselves.

The claim all over the Internet and in the media was that it drove out the healthy air and filled victims' lungs with Foul Air, which slowly congealed and hardened like concrete in your lungs and other organs. This could take weeks or even months. Or it could happen instantly. But who can believe news on the Internet?

IT WAS SAID THAT SILENT CARRIERS filled with Foul Air went stalking victims once it took control of their moral system. It was essentially a moral ailment. Never before in history had such a thing been seen, and humans had no immunity to it. It wasn't just that carriers—"Hunters" as they were called—were infected with Foul Air and might not realize it or were in denial about it, but that they purposely sought recruits and became quite literally predators upon their fellow man. This happened only after the ailment had progressed past the initial silent phase. Who could believe such a thing? Believe that the stricken chose to infect their own families? That they passed through grocery stores breathing Foul Air on packaged goods and vegetables, slinking along with cruel little smiles, knowing they would gain new recruits, much like vampires? Because, it was said, whoever touched what a Hunter had touched became infected. Some said college-age Hunters gathered on beaches among heedless young sunbathers. Moving their beach towels close to those still breathing good air, they would wink and nod at each other and pen healthy bathers in so they could not escape the Foul Air exhaled all around them. A pulmonologist in Milano said the world could expect to see more Hunters among the young than among older populations. Of course, he did not use the term "Hunters." No one in official positions did. He called them "positives." Positive in what way? There was no way to test who carried Foul Air and who didn't. No way to tell by looking at them—or so we thought early on.

But many rejected such thinking. As skeptical as people might be about others' capacity for goodness, most weren't ready to believe that parents would purposely endanger their own children. Thomas Sanchez, that enthusiastic doomsdayer, was infuriated by such thinking. "You know why the

Lord burned Sodom and Gomorrah, because the people were evil. You know why he condemned Cain to wander the earth in torment, because he killed his brother. Nah, righteousness is rewarded and evil is punished. God would never permit the slaughter of innocent children or defenseless elders."

This, after all, was during that time of elections when the candidates themselves, who all insisted they were negative, drew crowds of fanatic followers who breathed freely on one another, then fled out of auditoriums to breathe on others.

The Woman On The Corner was one of the first to report—first on Neighbor To Neighbor, then on social media—that the Hunters were accosting people on the street, wrestling them to the ground and breathing Foul Air directly into their mouths, pinching their noses closed as if performing mouth to mouth resuscitation on a drowning victim, except in this case suffocating them with Foul Air. Once their victims' cheeks puffed up like balloons, they released their nostrils, and good air hissed out of their noses while Foul Air filled their lungs. The Woman On The Corner claimed to have seen one tackling another neighbor and performing this ugly act of moral violation on her. Macy wondered if it was Mrs. Hernandez. Mr. Taylor said this was proof positive that the Woman On The Corner was off her head. "I never seen no one tackling anybody, and I walk maybe two hours every day. When does that woman ever leave her house? How she gonna see some air mugger or whatever the hell they are?" There were similar reports from Rome and Cairo and Beijing and, especially, New York: people seen tackling others in public and giving them mouth to mouth. But you expected that of New York even in normal times. Stock traders were said to tackle others on the trading floor, but they'd been doing that for years. It was a theory, anyway, that caught on mightily on the Internet, likely because it is a medium that thrives on paranoia. Some would say hate.

Still, early on, if they could have been counted, the deniers certainly outnumbered the alarmed. Isn't this always the case with bad news? We do not want to believe in calamity until we can no longer ignore it. If this weren't true, we would all be hiding under rocks. Young deniers congregated in large numbers in defiance of the Foul Air panic. "This is Y2K all over again," they insisted. "Much ado about nothing." "Man up, dude. You can't walk around scared all the time." "Hey, the air is bad everywhere. What else is new?"

Then came the epidemic of crows, hordes of them flying in tattered formation, scolding and squawking, rattling dice back in their throats as they occupied the branches of magnolia trees and weighed down palm fronds, staring hungrily down at us with their evil little black eyes. Upon seeing them, some people fled into their houses or cars, terrified when a murder of crows (as it is called) dive-bombed them. It was claimed the crows were conveyors of Foul Air; they thrived on it. "They's demons, you know," The Woman On The Corner said, "always has been. Just listen to them croak and tell me they don't sound like devils." She was constantly putting alarmist posts on Neighbor To Neighbor, which was once an informal community bulletin board noting street fairs and public meetings. There had always been an element of public anxiety on the site: reports of broken car windows and stolen batteries and young men going door to door with clipboards casing houses, so that if you read Neighbor To Neighbor regularly you would think the neighborhood was a war zone. Now Neighbor To Neighbor contributors posted the latest reports of Foul Air hotspots, certain alleys and stores you should avoid. Some small businesses were forced to close their doors after a few such posts.

Others, the lighthearted, the glass-half-fullers, fed and encouraged the crows. They threw out snacks for them in their backyards. The crows gathered in flocks, screeching and chasing each other away. It was a point of pride to these folks to have crows follow them, fleeting from tree to tree as they walked down the sidewalk or gliding slowly overhead like dark drones. It was total rot and bird bigotry, they said, to imagine crows breathed only Bad Air and carried it with them to contaminate entire blocks. They were beautiful creatures. Very smart. Very savvy. They knew more about human beings than humans knew about them. *That's precisely the trouble,* one of the fearful posted, *they know we are in trouble, and they're closing in on us.*

It was said that the Hunters lost their sense of taste and smell immediately after their lungs filled with Bad Air. This was why they were so hungry—at least appeared to be to the few who witnessed them and survived to tell about it. Smell and taste went long before their lungs began to harden, before they began to tackle people on the street and violate them orally. They were seemingly perfectly normal, mixing with others, including their own families, and suddenly found themselves unable to smell or taste. They become monstrously envious of those who retained their olfactory senses, even of their own mates and children. Grandmothers snatched food off the plates of their grandchildren and stuffed it ravenously into their mouths, thinking that it must be more nourishing than the tasteless food on their own plates, which was as bland as cardboard. The whole point of taste and smell is, after all, to whet the appetite. They seized their grandchildren by the back of the neck and pulled their faces close to peer into their eyes, thinking them secret carriers—or about to become so—because they recognized each other. Alarmed families locked such aggressive grannies in a back room to keep them from terrifying the children, only to find, a few days later, their children acting in much the same way: seizing food off plates with famished, hostile little smirks. Imagine what it must be to eat tasteless food. You would lose all desire to eat. No wonder they looked so hungry. No wonder crows followed people about, hopping from tree to tree in hopes they had a scrap of bread hidden in their pocket, prepared to assault them if they didn't give it up.

This was one of the greatest horrors of the Foul Air outbreak reported on social media. Entire families mistrusting one another, locked away in separate rooms so they couldn't accost each other. What became of such families? How were feeding arrangements managed? Access to bathrooms? No one could be sure because they didn't dare venture into such homes, notorious repositories of Foul Air. Not even the police would step inside when they received reports of domestic violence unless they were equipped with hazmat suits, which few were. There were reports of family members killing each other, even reports of domestic cannibalism. This can't be believed. We may at times be monstrous, but we aren't monsters. Although, a woman from Spain put up social media posts that went viral and were reported to have had more views than the Olympic Games, which went into great detail about how, first, their grandfather caught the Foul Air and seized food from his beloved grandkids' plates, then breathed Foul Air in their mouths. Who can believe such a thing? Then the six children ganged up on their father, who rapidly progressed through the stages of olfactory loss and other early symptoms of Bad Air, turning a greenish hue within four hours, his eyes gone hollow, his lungs, given the tortured way he was breathing, already beginning to clog up with mucousy cement. He chased his wife around the house. She holed up in a bedroom and pushed furniture against the door to keep him out. From there she delivered reports on social media to a fascinated, if horrified, world, placing her iPhone against the door so listeners could hear crows squawking outside and her husband's rants, plus occasional screeching outcries, either as if he was wringing the necks of crows and devouring them, feathers and all, or they were pecking greedily at him. At one point, we distinctly heard him collapse to the floor with a hollow thud. Poor man was a goner. Soon after that she said she was losing her sense of smell and pleaded with the world:

> Try to love one another, impossible as that seems in a time of hate. Confuse hate by turning it backwards into love. Stay away from others even if you are tortured by lack of touch. And, if you are young, avoid sex. God is testing us. Think of how much worse it could be: Sodom and Gomorrah or the Black Plague. God wants to learn if he made a mistake in creating us. He wantsto know if we can remain good and hopeful even on the doorstep of hell. He wants to know if we are still a creation made in his own image and has devised the Foul Air experiment to find out.

Some were moved by this. Others said it was sentimental rot. Still others that it was blasphemy. Many thought the whole thing was a fabrication, since it was generally accepted that the Hunters deliberately posted misinformation to mislead and terrify the public, telling them such and such a place was safe to hike, only to be waiting in the bushes to leap on hikers. Telling them that only those with hollow eyes could be trusted. That the best way to defeat the Bad Air was to congregate on beaches where fresh air blows in off the sea. That wearing half a coconut shell as a skull cap kept Bad Air away. This explained the run on coconuts.

Scientists generally applauded and seized upon the Spanish woman's account, for it suggested that the greater the infusion of Foul Air the more quickly the victim was overcome by it. They had suspected this. Now the father's rapid decline proved it. Her account was made especially potent by the low, soothing timbre of her voice, so calm and nearly angelic, making the horrors she was reporting seem all the more horrendous.

But it wasn't just Hunters who deliberately posted misinformation. There are three Devils, Willy Jefferson told his neighbor Hicks: *Uncertainty* (about "Bad Air" for example), *Fear* (the belief that good air everywhere is being supplanted by bad), and *Denial* (insistence there is nothing to worry about). "It's been that way throughout human history," he said. "Uncertainty, fear, and denial, the three potentates of human misery. The Bible is full of examples and great literature too. All three of them are hard at work now advocating for their position."

Beyond the coconut shells, there were other myths. Willy kept a list of them:

-Cow urine protects you from Bad Air (originating in India).

-Not a single surfer has been found with Foul Air Syndrome, because their lungs are full of good air coming off the sea (originating in California).

-Chili peppers drive Bad Air away (originating in Texas).

-Mockingbirds, which attack crows, are one of the heroes of the Bad Air epidemic (which seemed true enough to Willy).

-Foul air hangs above the houses of evil people, especially Democrats (originating, it is said, from a Baptist church in Florida).

-Bad air warps the air over Republican households (also concocted in California).

-Bad air is just good air gone bad.

This last was the most provocative, because it was true and said something profound about the nature of good and evil. Don't most people accept—all over the globe—that children are inherently innocent and good? It's only as they grow older that they lose their innocence and become acquainted with evil. Their good air goes bad.

This simple axiom sparked a worldwide campaign: SEQUESTER THE CHILDREN! Protect the innocent. Proponents suggested that if only we could sequester all the children in special structures built for that purpose, we could preserve their good air and prevent the bad from infecting them. It might have worked. But how long would they need to remain isolated? Weeks? Years? Their entire lives? There were heated arguments about this online.

Macy O'Brien, surprisingly, was a big advocate of SEQUESTER THE CHILDREN, possibly because she had no children of her own. While a fervid believer in population control, she was not anti-children. Rather she believed that only by limiting the birth of future children can we assure the well-being of those already born. Quixotically, she was also a fan of sci-fi novels that prophesize the imminent end of the world, which gave her common cause with Thomas Sanchez.

She stood on the sidewalk in front of his house while he sat on a lawn chair on his front porch, and they discussed what the Bible and sci-fi had in common: imminent disaster, the end of days, some lucky souls winging away to heaven or to distant planets, the near certainty that evil will eventually triumph over good, and so the world will end.

Poor Macy must dodge off the sidewalk into the street when passersby approached in case they were carrying Bad Air and didn't realize it, or they were among the deniers who made a point of walking close to others and breathing on them to express their skepticism, or they were, God forbid, secret Hunters. She sometimes had to run into the street to get away from them. None of them accosted Thomas since he had a shotgun leaning against the wall beside him and made it clear to everyone that he would use it. He offered to let Macy borrow his .357 magnum pistol, but she abhorred violence.

"You know what *The Book* says: 'permit the little children to come onto me and forbid them not,'" Thomas said. "I can't understand why people don't want to do that now. It's the only way to save the kids from evil."

"So you think it's not Foul Air but an epidemic of evil?"

He opened his hands. "It always has been."

She nodded thoughtfully. "Literature suggests as much. Or at least considers the idea. Dostoevsky was obsessed with it, so was Joseph Conrad."

"And Saint Augustine."

"You're right, Tom, him too. What about your Jesus?"

"My Jesus!" Thomas Sanchez tilted his chin upward as if listening for instructions from heaven. Macy was the only person outside his family he permitted to call him "Tom." "You're right...you're right. It's true. He may be the only person in history who believed good will ultimately triumph over evil. The only one. That's why people love him."

"How about Martin Luther King Jr. and Gandhi?"

He considered this. "Right! They were messengers. And Mother Teresa."

Generally though, people did not look to religion for comfort during the Foul Air crisis, not even in this unusually religious neighborhood. Maybe faith once helped to explain and justify human misery, but such explanations were no longer convincing, not in an age of science and prosperity when suffering seemed archaic. Belief might provide the faithful a simple explanation for Bad Air, as it did for Thomas Sanchez, but couldn't drive it away.

WILLY JEFFERSON STILL TALKED to his wife daily even though she had been dead for five years. She was one of the few people he ever talked to, which is to say he mostly spoke to the air. This made him singularly qualified to interrogate the Foul Air hypothesis. He told his wife Luella he was in a quandary about this whole Bad Air business, which had come to be known as "Foul Air Syndrome" or FAS. "I don't want to be a denier like Hicks next door. Well, you know the man. He believed 9/11 was a hoax perpetrated by the media and still does to this day. He believes this thing is a media invention too. Okay, maybe they've exaggerated it, but Hicks is a damn fool. You ask me, it's deniers like Hicks who are at greatest risk of catching FAS. At the other extreme we got the nut job up on the corner. Yeah, I know you're going to tell me she was brought up fearful and all and you feel sorry for her. But now the woman claims Hunters are camped on her front lawn, like a homeless encampment. I walk by there every morning and don't see nothing but her weed patch yard. I don't hold much water in this whole Hunter thing, anyway. Sounds like something Stephen King would cook up. Holding victims down on the ground and blowing Foul Air down their throats! That's cuckoo bird territory. So here's the question: Is there a middle ground between being either shit scared and living in denial? You understand what I'm saying? Yeah, I'm being careful; you don't need to worry about that. I go walking early in the morning. Look, I don't believe this crap about Hunters coming out at dusk, but why push my luck. Besides, there's no one out early and I value my privacy. I still sit out here to read. You know I won't give that up. A person needs some pleasures in life, else there's no reason to get up in the morning. You know I enjoy talking to you out here. Gets my day started. I don't even mind when Leroy or one of them walks by and asks how you're getting along and I can hear them grin. 'She doin' just fine, thank you, Leroy. How're you?'

"What I'm thinking, I should be helping out down at the food bank instead of sitting on my ass doing nothing. You understand? Now don't go on about how dangerous it would be. They don't have enough volunteers with so many people afraid of the Bad Air. I can wear a handkerchief over my mouth if you're worried. I'll look silly, but I'll do it. Gloves, too. I got to do something. Can't just stand by and watch it swallow us. You hear me? That's why I went to Nam. My country needed me. When all is said and done, some believe it's their duty to help out in bad times and some don't. There's volunteers and there's slackers. I'd like you to give it your blessing, Luella. The Bad Air might catch me up, but I'll go down fighting. Do nothing and my conscience will drag me down."

Meanwhile, Hicks next door was talking to his wife about how silly it was for people to be staying home from work. "If there's all this Foul Air people talk about, it could be anywhere: inside your house or right outside. No saying. Why would it be limited to people's places of employment? That don't make sense. If you ask me, it's a lot of propaganda, worse than the 9/11 hoax. Reminds me of the grassy knoll and all the conspiracy stuff after JFK's assassination."

MACY WAS TEACHING HER CLASSES online now, which suited her. She'd never liked lecturing. It was shyness that led her to be a bookworm as a girl and to choose reading as a way of life. Her students understood this and tolerated it, even stepped in to fill the void when she was having an off day, as a student did the last day of regular class. They were discussing Kafka's *The Trial*, and the girl asked if other students ever saw the world as Kafkaesque. "He's brilliant at describing what can't be described. Like what's happening now with FAS. It's surreal."

Another student told how a man had stopped his car mid-street and threw the door open to talk to him, ignoring other drivers who had to dodge around his car, honking their horns. "I'm not even sure he noticed. I was out for a run, and I stood on the sidewalk panting, trying to understand what he was saying. Something about a traffic ticket, and when he went to court no one was there. A sign on the Judge's bench said, 'in absentia.' Then he got another ticket which said his fine was doubled for failure to appear the first time, and he would face jail time if he failed to appear again. So he went back to the courthouse—that very morning—and it was closed. Poor dude was sucked right into *The Trial*. Still, he creeped me out. When I took off running again, he followed me, jabbering nonstop with his door standing wide open."

What Macy loved most about teaching was how students came to realize that we are all living in our own novels. Literature is an expression of everyday life. The question is always: How much do we write our own lives and how much are they written for us by outside events? All literature can be seen as an attempt to answer this question. It's an ongoing debate. Authors can be broadly divided into three categories:

–Deniers of Fate's final authority who believe character is fate, like Shakespeare.

–Those, like Flannery O'Connor and Kafka, who accept Fate's ultimate authority.

–Those who dodge back and forth between as if unable to make up their minds, like Mark Twain and Toni Morrison.

All three are viable positions. She saw students wrestle with this in their own lives, especially at a time like this, and found it gratifying to discuss it.

"So which type are you, Professor O'Brien?" the jogger asked her on that last day of meeting together in the classroom.

"Me?" The question caught her by surprise, and she realized she didn't have an answer. Perhaps this is why she taught literature rather than writing it, although it had been her childhood dream to become an author. The realization stunned her speechless.

The girl who usually stepped in and took over when she was feeling off, proclaimed, "It's pretty obvious. Macy is an in-betweener; she doesn't favor one type of writer over another. That's why I love this class."

Macy was particularly afraid to ride the metro home that evening, even though she lived only two stops from USC and there were few people on the train. There was an ongoing debate about how long Bad Air remained in an enclosed space after a carrier had passed through. Some claimed that it could remain for weeks; others found this preposterous. Foul air always disappears. Consider the smell of cooking in a kitchen. It dissipates even when the windows are closed. What becomes of it? Does it seep into the walls or fall to the floor? Do we inhale and reprocess it? This worried her on that trip home. Was she reprocessing Bad Air?

She emailed her dean that evening: *I will be canceling my in situ classes, Dean Whitlock. I understand the university hasn't yet come to this decision, but I feel it's the responsible thing to do. If I'm penalized, so be it. We will meet online until further notice.* She also decided that evening that she would write a novel titled FEAR OF BREATHING while she was in seclusion, and realized moreover that she was not an in-betweener at all but firmly in Flannery O'Connor's camp. Fate is the great determiner. Here was proof of it: FAS was providing her an opportunity to write a novel, so she would do it. She was up until four a.m. She wrote fifty pages, then fell asleep with her head on the desk, exhausted.

The next morning, an op-ed appeared in the *New York Times* arguing that the Foul Air Epidemic was a result of global warming. Animals like polar bears and bats were being forced out of their natural habitats and invading the habitats of other species, like grizzly bears and humans, while humans had invaded the habitats of hundreds of species that had once lived at a distance. *These invasive species minutely change the air's chemistry so that indigenous inhabitants are put at risk, as are the invaders. Our environment is becoming somewhat more anoxic, and those mediums that once enabled us to thrive, air and water, are slowly becoming toxic to us. We can expect an explosion of anaerobic organisms unparalleled for over three billion years.* The author was proposing that humans are going to be replaced by bacteria.

When, bleary-eyed, Macy read the article late that morning, she understood that she was writing a post-apocalyptic sci-fi novel and that she had already prophesied what this scientist was proposing. Perhaps she was the genius that she had always believed she wasn't. The idea unnerved her.

Thomas Sanchez was also thinking along apocalyptic lines and spoke to Macy about it when she passed on her walk that afternoon. "Suppose this Bad Air hangs around a while like they predict. People will stop mating, you know. They'll want to keep their distance. My wife is already refusing to stay in the same room with me."

"Maybe that's a good thing. No...I mean...not you…I didn't mean...not your wife, Tom. I mean having fewer children. Maybe the world needs that."

"God wants us to have more children, not less. He commanded us to be fruitful and multiply."

"Yes...well, maybe...a long time ago. I'm not sure it still applies."

Macy observed that The Woman On The Corner had posted no trespassing signs on her front lawn. She was spraying the grass with Roundup when Macy walked by. "That kills the grass, you know," Macy said from a safe distance.

"I wanna kill it. The Hunters won't like it here so much if the grass is dead," The Woman said. "They's still human even if they don't act human." Macy realized she would have to base a character on The Woman On The Corner: she epitomized something. She was infected with fear. Also realized that she was being much more assertive than usual. Maybe writing was emboldening her.

A CROW HAD BEEN PERCHED for two days on the head of the life-like owl decoy mounted high atop a pole overlooking the vegetable garden in Willy's backyard, meant to scare birds away, but this crow wasn't impressed. It made Willy nervous. What kind of bird was this? Other crows kept their distance, scolding the owl from the palm tree out front of his house. Maybe they were afraid of the defiant crow, too, sensing it was infected with Foul Air. Crow social distancing. The idea amused him. The bird's BB eyes fixed on him. "What's your problem? You eating my strawberries?" He considered walking up and shaking the pole to shoo the bird away, but it seemed prudent to keep his distance, as he did from people lately. Perhaps this was a Hunter in the guise of a bird. Possibly there were Hunters among many species. He might throw a rock at it, but if he hit and killed it he would have to get close to dispose of its body. Besides, he didn't want to harm it if it was a normal bird, a fellow animal with every right to live. It might even be Luella paying him a visit in another incarnation. She could be bossy and obstinate like a crow; she had always been fond of them. "Not saying you are," he told the bird. "Just that you could be. Isn't no harm in talking to a bird anyhow."

"I went to the food bank. I wore a mask and latex gloves like I promised you. They told me to come back in two weeks after I self-quarantined. I told them I already did. They said another two for safety's sake. I could see they were overwhelmed: people stretched out the door and around the block. Whole families. A line of cars maybe a quarter mile long. It was like a scene out of the depression. Everyone out of work, out of money. The priest in charge saw me looking and shook his head. 'All this from a threat we can't see and can't be sure is real.'"

"'Oh, it's real enough all right. Real as a heart attack,' I told him. He said he never thought he'd live to see anything like this, which surprised me since he sees it every day: people without a roof over their head or enough to eat. Maybe not so many. 'That's different,' he said. 'That's man-made. This is an act of God. We can't see it; we don't know how big it's going to get or when it will end. It's the great unknowable.' I said the worst things are always the ones we can't see, 'cause what we can't see we can't avoid. Anyway, if I'm still here in two weeks I'll go back." The bird shifted on its perch, causing the owl's head to bobble. Like it was asking Willy why he thought he might not be here in two weeks or how he could assume he would be.

"I've lived through worse. I'm a survivor. Sometimes I wish I wasn't, but I am."

At that, the bird leapt off its perch and winged straight for him, hovering two feet over his head with a great flurry of wings. Willy ducked and covered. His dog Jackal, who'd been lying beside him paying close attention to the bird as if sensing it was something more than a bird, leapt for it, barking and snapping. Willy fled to the house with hands shielding his head, Jackal on his heels. He slammed the door closed behind them. His heart was racing; he hadn't been this shaken since the Tet Offensive in Vietnam.

"Damn thing got too close. It isn't no Luella. I don't know if you're full of Bad Air," he said, looking out the window at it, "but you're flying in it sure enough. I could feel it under your wings. Reminded me of the air over in 'Nam, moldy jungle air. Death air." He could feel it clinging to the skin under his shirt, fetid and greasy. The bird was hovering just beyond the glass, treading air and glaring in at him with a primitive anger that was like nothing he'd ever seen. He feared it would break the glass to get at him. Its eyes black and glassy as obsidian, forged in some angry fire from days when the earth was still molten rock. An omen, perhaps, that the world was turning molten again. He thought to get his gun from under the bed and blow the damn thing out of the air. But who knew what evil would spew out with its guts. He clapped his hands to chase it off. The bird flew over to perch on the back of the chair he'd been sitting in. It rubbed its beak against the fabric, inhaling what little of him remained behind. "What do you think it wants?" he asked Jackal. "Do they want to replace our good air with their bad? Is it some kind of hunger you think? One thing's sure: I'll have to quarantine for two weeks now whether I want to or not. I may be contaminated." In all his reading about zoology, one of his favorite subjects, he'd never heard of an animal behaving this way.

Willy Jefferson was a self-educated man. He'd come west with his family from Alabama when he was fifteen. Some said Willy was one of the brave Black children who first integrated schools in Montgomery. He was beaten for it and his family targeted with death threats. So they fled west. He carried a silent dignity about him, like one who'd acquitted himself well in battle and took quiet pride in it. He had two years of college, but poverty made it impossible for him to finish. He enlisted and went to fight in Vietnam, where he acquitted himself well in battle again. Despite not graduating from college, he was well-educated, primarily self-taught, a voracious reader, always sitting out on his porch with a book. Folks would stroll past and call out to him, seeing only the top of his head beyond the low wall enclosing the porch, "Morning, Willy. What you reading today?" "Proudhon," he would say or "Thomas Mann," neither of whom they'd ever heard of. He loved novellas and had made it his task to read every one ever written in English and the three languages he'd taught himself: Spanish, French, and Italian. Macy shared his love of reading and sometimes sat on the porch talking books with him. "Did your wife like to read?" she once asked.

"Nah, she loved to cook and garden. She kept my feet on the ground. Since she left me, I sometimes feel I'm going to float away."

"I know the feeling," she said. "Maybe it's living inside your head so much. Or loneliness."

It impressed him how honest Macy was, given her shyness. He once considered dating her, but she wasn't his type. High strung and fussy, skinny as a pole. He liked women with their feet on the ground and some flesh on their bones. He told her to let him know if she ever needed anything. "If anyone ever gives you grief."

"Who's going to give me grief? I feel perfectly safe here."

He realized he no longer did, intuiting that the comfort and security people took for granted was a thin glaze that concealed something ominous beneath, which was bound to break out one day like a hidden fever. Maybe that day had come.

MACY CONTINUED WRITING at that initial frantic pace for five straight days: 240 pages. When students contacted her, anxious to see how they had fared on their last essay, she sent a group email: *Sorry, I will be indisposed for the next few days. I have been overtaken by something beyond my control.*

Not Foul Air, not to worry. I will have your papers graded by next week. At this rate, she realized, she would finish a draft of the book in a week. Then what? Start another? Maybe she would produce book after book, a string of them that had been queued up inside her for years, waiting to be born.

She found herself drawn to Willy's porch when she took her afternoon walk, since he and Thomas Sanchez were the only other readers in the neighborhood, though Thomas read only religious texts. Approaching, she saw that Willy had hung bird netting around the porch, completely enclosing it. "Is that you, Willy?" she asked a shadowy figure sitting inside.

"You can slip underneath," he said. "I'm trying to keep crows out, one crow in particular."

She crawled under the netting and sat in the second chair. "Guess what! I'm writing a novel," she said proudly.

He reached over to bump knuckles with her, maintaining the distance recommended by medical authorities to keep from breathing Foul Air should a person be a secret carrier. Macy could not imagine this of Willy, since he was the opposite of secretive. Whatever he was thinking was instantly on his lips. But how could she be sure she wasn't? No one could.

"What's this masterpiece-in-the-making about?" Willy asked.

"I think it's about how we can't trust ourselves or anyone else anymore. We don't know what evil we may be carrying inside us, nobody does."

"What do you mean you 'think it's about?' If you're writing a book, shouldn't you know what it's about?"

"That's the part I didn't understand until now," she said excitedly. "How authors, even great authors, have to discover what they are writing about as they go. They often don't know in advance. I never understood that. Now that I'm doing it, it seems obvious. It's more an unconscious than a conscious process. Very exciting. Very invigorating."

Willy shook his head. "Sounds like mumbo jumbo to me."

"In a way, yes. Or call it *magic*," she cried. "I had no idea that the people in my novel who migrate to a remote island from all over the world, drawn by a mysterious force, all share a genetic defect they didn't know they had until they arrive on the island and bring it out in each other, like an infection."

"Science fiction," Willy said. "Maybe an allegory?"

"I knew they had lost faith in modern civilization and longed to return to nature. They realized that civilization is an empty promise that leads people to despair and is destroying the earth, and all felt this deep longing to escape it, but they had no idea what that would lead to. Neither did I."

"So what happens?"

"On the island? They all turn into anaerobic bacteria, primitive, non-air breathing single-celled organisms."

Willy guffawed and slapped his thighs. "Damn!" Then put a finger to his lips. "Shhhhh. We don't want to alert it we're here," he whispered.

"Your crow?" The crow business didn't surprise her. Willy would read a book or watch a movie and live in it for days after. Likely, he'd recently seen Hitchcock's *The Birds*. After reading *Crime and Punishment*, he collected all his weapons—guns, knives, and a hatchet—and locked them away in a cupboard in the garage and gave the key to Hicks next door. "So if I have a sudden urge to kill someone I won't have the means." God help him if he rewatched *The Night of the Living Dead*. But weren't they all living in that movie at the moment?

"They lead a much simpler life as single-celled humans," she continued. "They are all alike, no genders, no races. They reproduce by mitosis. They split in two, which I've always thought the most hygienic form of reproduction."

Willy laughed again. "You want to split in two?"

"My characters seem to like it. They are much more self-sufficient than in their previous lives, even though they're all exactly alike."

Willy nodded. Macy was writing about herself, as he suspected all writers did. He and Luella used to talk about how Macy emitted no sexual vibes whatever; she was as asexual as her human bacteria. Luella believed she was still a virgin or at least wanted to be.

"Because they're all exactly alike they don't have any prejudices," she continued. "They're all equals. They share a genetic code which allows them to revert to single-celled organisms, and this evolutionary leap joins them in common cause."

"A leap backwards," Willy said, "reverse evolution to a more primitive life form."

"It's significant that they are anaerobic; the air is toxic to them, oxygen is. They don't dare breathe it. They must burrow deep into the island's bogs to survive."

"Toxic air! Sounds familiar. So you've been inspired by current events?"

"I suppose so. I hadn't considered it. What matters is they are happy living in the muck on their far-away island. A simple life close to the earth. They begin to trust themselves and one another again which they no longer could as humans."

Willy studied her for a time. She was onto something. You couldn't help thinking this Bad Air business and the panic attending it was the product of an age of indulgence wherein people had lost track of what was truly essential. Baba Ram Baba in West Hollywood called it "a crisis of spiritual identity." Thomas Sanchez regularly echoed that belief: "People don't know who they are anymore."

"It's a theme lately: people metamorphosing into alien life forms," Willy said. "I'm not sure what it signifies. Discontent maybe."

"We are disappointed in ourselves," Macy said.

"Luella was always saying how people try one fad after another and never do find contentment. I suppose we're defective that way."

That evening, something tapped at Macy's office window while she was grading papers. She froze to listen. There were reports on Neighbor To Neighbor of unscrupulous people taking advantage of the crisis to prey on others, especially those living alone. A gang of teenage boys tapped at people's doors and windows in the middle of the night like Hunters were said to do, just to frighten them. Surely they knew she lived alone, a defenseless middle-aged woman. She now wished she had taken Tom's pistol. Flushed with anger and emboldened by her recent foray into creativity, she went to the window and threw open the curtains. Instead of a group of teenage boys peering in at her, she saw what might have been Poe's raven: huge, wild-eyed, standing on the sill pecking at the glass with its curved beak. "What do you want?" she shouted. "Shoo!" Waving hands at it. Remarkably the crow flew away with a series of loud croaks.

She put aside student papers and began writing in a fury:

> *Things had become discombobulated, confused, chaotic. Foul air, which was to say air infused with oxygen, somehow invaded their anaerobic sloughs and caused the microbe people to choke and gasp and eventually drown. Their tiny, ravaged bodies floated to the oily surface by the millions.*

Macy realized that she had just written the book's climax. It caught her by surprise. She wasn't sure it was ready to climax yet. How could you know? In life, we never know events have reached a climax until we see them in retrospect. FAS, for example; how would anyone know when it had reached its zenith and was headed toward the last chapter?

RUMORS ABOUNDED. SOME SAID family pets were being infected with Foul Air and could pass it on to their owners. And vice versa. Sitting on the couch one evening side by side, Willy and Jackal exchanged a wary glance. Perhaps dogs had their grapevine too, and the rumor was passing around among them. They could both confirm the truth of another rumor: Hunters roamed the streets late at night. Willy always cracked open the drapes and peered out the living room window for a few minutes before going to bed. Jackal looked out at his feet. Along with passing raccoons and feral cats, they sometimes saw slumped, hooded beings slouching along mid-street, throwing predatory glances side to side, eyes aglow like tiny, penetrating lasers. Willy would leap away from the window, hoping they hadn't seen him.

Almost everyone wore masks now, even though the experts claimed they were of no use against Foul Air, which always found a way to creep around their edges or pass through the weave. When people saw anyone not wearing one, they made tsk-tsk-tsk sounds. There was even a special section on Neighbor To Neighbor called "The TSK-TSK-TSK Registry," which encouraged people to report neighbors who refused to mask up. Macy thought it smacked of authoritarianism. She knew that authority thrives on tragedy. During good times it becomes all but irrelevant.

The Woman On The Corner had barricaded herself inside her house, nailing boards over the windows. Her neighbor, Mr. Taylor, suspected she lay dead inside. Willy promised Luella he would check on her but dreaded doing so. Perhaps it was right and responsible to check on a neighbor in need. But sometimes what is right and responsible isn't wise. What would he do, for instance, if after knocking repeatedly on all her doors and windows there was no answer? Should he break in and enter what might be a miasma of Foul Air to check on her, not only exposing himself but letting it spill out into the neighborhood? It was said that the longer Foul Air remained in a closed space the more concentrated it became, like propane gas leaking from a stove. It might be noble and honorable to put others above yourself. He believed it was why he went to 'Nam as a young man, placing country above self. But that war had turned out to be a disaster. Still, to always put yourself first was no answer. He could not in good conscience remain holed up in a crisis when he could be out helping the less fortunate. "Here I am," he complained to Luella, "trapped between my own well-being and the well-being of others. It's a conundrum. I want to do what's right, but I'm not sure what that is at a time like this."

"You worry too much," she would have told him if she'd been there.

The next day, a group of deniers up the street past The Woman On The Corner's House held a block party on their front lawns, complete with canopies, tables, beer, barbecued ribs, and "Jesus saves" music blaring across the neighborhood from huge speakers. A large banner proclaimed *The Lord will protect us*. Willy thought this a hollow philosophy during a time of crisis when no one, neither believers nor nonbelievers, was spared. The Lord wasn't offering his followers much protection. It annoyed him that they should be proselytizing, urging residents to come out and party in defiance of the general agreement that social distancing limited the transmittal of FAS. Few joined them. Most people out walking their dogs dodged across the street, frowning at the revelers and muttering disapproval. However, many young folks walked obliviously past, eyes glued to their iPhone screens, totally unaware of social distancing. Insulation from the real world is another form of denial, Willy realized, which put them in great peril. He stood out on his lawn shaking his head, quietly cursing their fools' rebellion. One fellow he often saw walking his two big German Shepherds stood mid-street cursing the revelers, his dogs lunging toward them. They laughed and raised beer bottles to toast him.

Seeing Hicks walk out to his car, Willy called to him, "Can you believe this, Hicks? Putting everyone in the neighborhood at risk, including their own kids and grandmas. Damn fools. There's going to be violence. Guaranteed. There's always violence when people are stressed."

Hicks didn't look so good. He walked stiffly as an old man, was wan and gloomy, like a cloud had settled over him. He stood a minute at his car door absent-mindedly fumbling with his keys. "I've got my own troubles, man," he mumbled. "I got laid off. Company's closing up shop. Insurance is gone belly up with all the Foul Air claims and no one buying policies. They say isn't no insurance can protect you from Bad Air no matter how much you pay for it. That's where fear gets us, Willy. Panic. Economic stagnation. Everybody's giving up common sense over what they can't see and can't be sure is even there. It's crazy."

"Sorry to hear it, Hicks." Gesturing at the celebration down the street, a man shouting over the loudspeakers that it was time for people to drop to their knees and pray for deliverance. "Maybe I can understand the praying part. There were guys in 'Nam would pray every time we went on patrol. No atheists in a foxhole, right? I did myself sometimes; I considered it prophylaxis, like taking my saline tablets. But the fools who dropped to their knees when we were in a fire fight were a danger to everyone, like those fools up the street."

Hicks' eyes roamed toward the celebration on the next block. "I may join them. I could use some cheering up. Times like these, you got to have some hope even if it makes you a fool."

Willy wondered why scientific rationality is at bottom of the list where belief is concerned. People prefer myths to facts. Just then an LAPD copter buzzed low overhead on its way to some disaster. Willy ducked and clasped hands over his head as always when a Dust Off flew over, an instinct carried over from the long-ago war. He realized it was the first helicopter he'd heard all day. Typically, there were a dozen or so. After it had passed, he thought he detected a slight distortion of air up on the next block. Ridiculous. He wasn't going there.

Macy was just then passing The Woman On The Corner's house. She'd left a note on her door asking her to call if she needed anything. Poor thing, terrified and alone. Then she realized she was in the same position, though wasn't seemingly as frightened. Why was that? And why were her neighbors throwing a party? Celebrating what? A couple of dozen revelers laughed and shouted boisterously. They started a line dance, a wiggling snake that wended down the sidewalk. Foul air snake. *Eat, drink and be merry, for tomorrow we die.* But she wasn't sure whether her neighbors were welcoming death or defying it. Besides, no one was certain that Foul Air victims did die. Upon first arriving at hospitals, they lay for some time struggling to expel Foul Air, looking desperately up at their doctors. After a time of convalescence, the infected seized medical personnel by the throat, rode them to the floor and blew Bad Air into their lungs, so it was reported, then fled the hospital. Infected medical workers repeated this pattern and became Hunters of their colleagues until there were few medical personnel left, and many hospitals were forced to close their doors. It led to a revival of that old children's ditty from the time of the Spanish flu:

> I had a little bird, its name was Enza,
> I opened the window and in-flu-Enza.

Revised to:

> I once knew a Doctor whose name was Fowler,
> when he got to the hospital it changed to Foulair.

People chanted it as an incantation whenever they passed a hospital, most boarded up now, too dangerous to enter. A few brave medical staff tended to rows of patients lined up on gurneys in hospital parking lots.

What became of those infected with Foul Air? So many theories. Surely they went off somewhere to die, deep into the forest perhaps. Or they rose, as some claimed, into the air. Or they popped and vanished, leaving small puffs of toxic air behind. Or wandered the streets at night like vampires, famished, driven by blood lust, seeking their next victim. The Woman On The Corner had seen them encamped on her front lawn, and Willy had seen them shuffling along the street late at night. But maybe those were just people fed up with confinement who needed to get out for a stroll.

THERE WAS NO SAYING WHEN the intruder arrived, possibly during the night or early that morning before Willy woke up. Surprisingly, Jackal didn't sound the alarm as he usually did when a stranger approached the house: a single startling bark. Perhaps the trespasser was very quiet. Willy was in the kitchen making coffee when he heard Jackal snarling at the front door.

"What the hell, Jacko? Someone at the door?"

Instinct stopped him from throwing the door wide open as he usually did, ready to give a hearty welcome to a neighbor or point at the "no soliciting" sign if it was a solicitor and bark, "Get the hell off my porch. Can't you read?" They always carried clipboards, thinking it made them look official. He cracked the door open just enough to peek out through the reinforced screen door. After the Rodney King riots, most residents had installed solid steel doors with thick metal mesh impenetrable to anything but a cutting torch, along with bars over the windows, since some rioters trashed their own neighborhoods. Willy was alarmed to see a man sitting in the lawn chair where he usually sat reading, turning abruptly to him when he opened the door. "What the hell?" Willy began, about to unleash a volley of curses, but something about the man's distorted face made him hesitate. Jackal growled low in his throat, teeth bared, lunging at the door, then backing off and scratching at the hardwood floor as he retreated. "Damn, Jacko, take it easy." Willy had never seen his dog show fear; he could be quite menacing.

The stranger's face was blurred, no doubt due to the steel mesh, his image pixelated so that the mind must fill in the blanks to make sense of it. But Willy's mind couldn't make sense of what it saw: the face blurred but not the body. The intruder's legs outstretched, his feet planted on a five gallon bucket Willy kept out front to wash the car. He wore scrappy tennis shoes, tattered khaki pants, a grease-stained hoodie bearing the logo: "All For One / And One For All." Odd slogan for a homeless man to boast, he thought. Then again, maybe it wasn't. And why assume he was homeless? Who else would have the audacity to sit in his chair? Yolanda down the street once found an entire family camped on her porch and shooed them away with a broom. Perhaps he doesn't realize he's violating my space, Willy thought, since the stranger's demeanor asked, "What you looking at?" Or he was mentally ill, as many were said to be. You'd expect a homeless man to have a garbage bag stuffed with belongings at his side. Or a grocery cart out on the sidewalk. Opening the door wider, Willy didn't see one. He wanted the intruder to see that he was a large man and Jackal was growling nonstop at his side.

The trespasser's face was generic, genderless, neither young nor old, but not abstract, not featureless, rather the features were coarse and exaggerated, right out of a *Comedia dell'arte* bestiary: huge eyes, gaping nostrils, skin wrinkled as a prune from forehead to mottled neck—minutely wrinkled as if all the worries of the ages rested on his shoulders. As if, like Cain, the creature must wander the earth from pillar to post. Perhaps "he" wasn't the correct pronoun to apply to the trespasser, for Willy sensed that this being wasn't strictly human, maybe not human at all except in form. The correct pronoun may well have been "it." This sent a shiver down his spine.

Willy closed the door and leaned back against it, gripping his elbows and breathing. "What the hell, Jacko! Who... what's that, boy? Scared the hell outta me." Willy didn't scare easily. As a teenager, he'd helped integrate schools in Montgomery, Alabama. After his first tour of duty in 'Nam, he re-upped (his buddies thought him crazy); he survived the

Tet Offensive, was on the Selma March back in the day and faced down crackers who spit in his face without flinching; he'd once nearly died of pneumonia, which left his lungs scarred before it moved on to the next poor bastard, because that's what ailments do: they hunt down their victims, roam streets and hospital wards seeking the vulnerable, much like lions cull the weak from zebra herds. He'd once seized the blade of a knife that a mugger brandished at him outside the liquor store on the corner of Jefferson; it nearly sliced off a finger. The only thing that had ever truly frightened him was Luella's breast cancer. And now this...whatever it was.

Some threats, he knew, are limited, like a toothache; we can fathom the extent of the damage they're likely to do. Some are unlimited, like a stock market crash; the potential damage isn't readily knowable, but we know it will ultimately end. Worst of all are the existential threats, like Luella's cancer, which are totally life-altering and unfathomable to us. The intruder seemed of this third kind.

"What we're going to do—" he whispered to Jackal who regarded him quizzically, likely wondering why he was whispering and why he didn't chase the intruder away "—we're going to leave him sit a while. No harm done, right? We'll come back in half an hour and see if he's gone, which he likely will be. Chase the bastard off if he isn't. That okay with you?" Jackal whined.

Willy fixed him a bowl of kibble with a bit of wet food mixed in. "Only two days' worth left," he warned. "Hope they'll have restocked the shelves." Only half a bowl of granola left for him. No bananas. No milk. No one knew why the stores were out of most staples. They were facing Foul Air, not a food shortage, not a hurricane that disrupted the supply chain. It didn't make sense, but nothing did lately.

Granola with water didn't cut it. Neither of them was much in the mood to eat anyway. Their thoughts were out on the front porch.

He went into the backyard to check the ruby red semi-dwarf grapefruit he'd just planted. A little nervous going out, looking this way and that, asking himself, "What's the problem? You worried the bastard has an evil twin or something?" He couldn't likely have scaled the fence since it was eight feet high. Still, Willy patrolled the yard as if walking point, peering cautiously around corners of the garage and storage shed and into the garden. His son Justin would have ragged him about it. "Whassup, Pop? You look like a spooked rabbit out here."

Sometimes there's good reason to be spooked.

Jackal sniffed at the bottom of the steel gate on the south side of the house, vacuuming up smells from the space where it met the ground. "Isn't gone yet?" Willy asked him. "What d'you suppose he wants?" Something more, he knew, than the recyclable cans and bottles homeless scavengers dug out of recycling bins. Willy had once chased them off, until Denny Tibbs admonished him, "What it cost you, man? The brother recycles bottles you toss out to buy him a slice of pizza. Always put your trash back in the bin, don't they? You doing them a good deed and don't cost you nothing." So he let them take it.

Now and again, some poor wretch took a drink of water from the spigot by the front porch. He couldn't begrudge them that. Everyone gets thirsty. But he got howling mad the time a man took a dump in his driveway and Willy stepped in it chasing him off the property, stood with his foot stuck in a mound of human excrement left by a stranger, which was sucking the sneaker off his foot. He ran into the house to get his revolver from under the bed, tracking excrement across the floor behind him, and chased the man down the street, with Luella shouting after him: "Willy, are you crazy? Get back here with that gun." After scrubbing the floor, he threw his brand new Nike sneakers in the trash.

He ran the speech he would deliver to the man on the porch (if it was a man) past Luella, seeking her anger management advice. No telling what he might say if left on his own.

> "All right, brother. I know it's hard times. Nervous times. People saying they never experienced nothing like it. We're all in this together, so I got nothing personal against you sitting on my porch. All right? But there's a principle here, you understand? It's my porch, and I ought to have some say in who uses it. Besides, I like to sit out mornings reading a book and talking to my wife. Let's say you have a bag of crushed cans sitting beside you on the sidewalk, do I have a rightto make off with it, brother? You gonna say I'm not using the porch just now and you're only borrowing it. I understand. Under normal circumstances, I'd say, 'No problem.' But these aren't normal times, brother. Man, I don't know if you're carrying Bad Air and you don't know if I am. I can't squeeze by you to get the mail without coming too close, you understand? Besides, I'm not sure of your intentions. Maybe if we could work that part out we could come to an agreement. Fair enough?"

Jackal cocked his head as dogs will do, as if to ask, "All that, really?"

"Just trying to find the proper tone." Because it struck him that this intruder might be one of the folks he would be helping to feed down at the food bank once he'd finished his quarantine. This was practice for that time. He didn't want to get off on the wrong foot. Call it a test run, right down to maintaining proper distancing.

Returning to the house, he held a finger to his lips for Jackal to keep quiet. As they approached the front door, he experienced that shiver of fear he'd felt earlier and admonished himself, "Nothing to worry about. Just some sad, homeless bastard taking a breather." To be on the safe side, he tied one of Luella's old scarves around his neck like a bandana to cover his nose and mouth. Still, he hesitated before turning the knob. It was like passing a lurking cop car doing 85 in a 65 zone; you dreaded looking in the rearview for fear you'd see red lights flashing behind you. Willy shut his eyes as he cracked the door open, hoping the intruder would be gone. He wasn't.

He was asleep it seemed, eyelids closed like shutters, smooth as a lizard's, contrasting the wrinkled skin of his face. He was draped wantonly over the chair waiting for him, Willy knew, biding his time. No chance he could get past him without tripping over his legs. Anger hit him like the palm of a hand against his forehead. He opened the screen door wide and shouted, "Y'r on my damn porch, man. Y'r fucking trespassing. Get moving."

The man's lizard eyelashes rolled slowly upward like an old-fashioned scroll top desk; dark eyes fixed Willy without expression. If eyes are windows on the soul, his were windows on an empty room.

"Go on. Git!" Shooing him away with a hand. "You want me to call the police?"

One corner of the intruder's mouth lifted in what wasn't quite a smile. He didn't speak—maybe couldn't—nonetheless, somewhere deep in his brain Willy heard him say, *The police don't worry me none*, as if the creature's mind had invaded his. It placed its hands on the chair arms as if to stand up. "Damn you!" Willy leapt back behind the steel door and threw the latch, snatched his hand away as if it had given him a shock. He stepped away from the door, fearing the creature would put his face against the mesh and blow Foul Air at him, but it remained frozen in that tense pose as if preparing to rise. *I'm here*, Willy heard him say without speaking. Jackal heard it too and barked furiously at him through the steel mesh, whined, backed away, then rushed forward to bark again.

How close did you dare be to one of these so-called Hunters? Six feet? Ten? One-hundred? He was too close. Willy closed the heavy inner door, ran to the bathroom and scrubbed his hands for a good minute, then brushed his tongue with a soapy toothbrush. Couldn't say why. He hadn't touched the creature. It just seemed prudent. Admonishing himself, "This is silly. Go out with the gun and chase him off. He's got no right to be there...except maybe he does. That's the trouble! Nothing's certain anymore. Not security, not property, not common sense...nothing. Not even good air. Everything's on loan."

Nonetheless, he marched through the living room, gun in hand, Jackal on his heels, threw open the door and confronted the beast with the revolver. The creature stood up to greet him, not six feet away. His face remained blurred even without the intervening steel mesh, undulating as if heat waves washed over it. But not the body. Willy grabbed Jackal's collar as he rushed past him to attack the beast; the dog nearly pulled him off his feet. He just managed to slam the screen door shut before the creature stepped inside, then the heavy oak door behind it. That last image of the beast was one that would remain embedded in his mind and keep him awake at night as images from 'Nam had done for years, projected against the dark walls of the bedroom. The creature's mouth yawning open, teeth oddly spiked—like toadstools, with thin stalks and wide caps. Something hideous hung at back of his throat, seething as if flies swarmed over it. The empty eyes reflected cold, metallic light back at him. Whatever life the thing possessed was not animal life. And the smell! Like the catarrhal smell of bronchitis amplified many times over. The odor of Foul Air perhaps. Foul air was sitting on his front porch. It had come for him.

He retreated with Jackal to the backyard and gargled repeatedly with hot water from the utility sink faucet, having heard that hot liquid neutralizes Bad Air. Many things were said to do so. Some wore amulets of woven hemp around their necks, others rubbed aloe vera on their faces. Russian Orthodox believers drove the empty streets sprinkling holy water to keep it at bay. All of it nonsense, Willy knew, but also knew that in the face of such an existential threat we will try anything to comfort ourselves. In 'Nam, the boys fired into the air for a mad minute before turning in, hoping to keep Charlie at bay—but actually betraying their whereabouts to him. During an earthquake in Mexico City years ago, a terrified man had knelt in the street to pray for mercy and was run down by a bus, the only casualty resulting from that quake. Action, whether sensible or not, gives us hope. He'd come far too close to that monster and was likely done for.

"It's all right," he assured Jackal, who had been nearly overwhelmed by the stench given his acute sense of smell. "Give it a little time and the smell will dissipate. It hangs in the air for a while. We should stay out of the living room for a few days until it leaves."

SOME PEOPLE HAD TAKEN TO SINGING late at night. You couldn't make out the words or tell where they came from. Some said the practice began in Italy and spread across Europe, then over much of the globe. The choir we were hearing was a world chorus. Tens of millions of voices lifted to the sky at the same moment, asking for protection from Bad Air and a return to normalcy. Some thought they heard John Lennon's "Imagine" on the wind or the Hallelujah Chorus. It sounded to Macy like dozens of melodies woven into a single musical quilt, lyrical and haunting, a celestial hum. Magical, really. Ethereal. She would sit out in her backyard at night listening. It gave her a sense of peace and connection in those troubled times. She sometimes heard voices from the church down on the corner of Jefferson join in. It was said that four of the congregants had come down with Foul Air, but that didn't discourage the others from singing. In fact, it made them sing more fervently. Mrs. Johnson, a street over, sang gospel songs in a vibrant contralto reminiscent of Mahalia Jackson, "Nearer My God To Thee" and others she recognized. It's curious how tragedy brings out the best in us, Macy thought. Perhaps if we suffered disaster every day of our lives we would be better people. But, sadly, it brings out the worst in us as well.

She realized that she shouldn't be sitting outside, given reports of Hunters lurking about at night, although this was likely just another social media scare. Even if it was true, they wouldn't expect her to be sitting outside in her yard rather than hidden behind locked doors. She found it inspiring to gaze up at the moon. The night sky was darker and stars brighter since Bad Air had closed things down. People saw wild animals roaming the streets of the city now that people were staying mostly inside. This made her all the more certain that this contagion of Bad Air was related to global warming. A foreshadowing of future times when city lights would begin to blink off for good and the nights would return to primordial darkness. She must work this into her novel. There would, of course, be many plagues and pandemics of zoonotic diseases passed between animals and people, along with rising seawater and warmer temperatures. A return to tropical conditions would breed many exotic ailments unknown to man. This was partly why the people on her island had devolved into single-celled organisms. Primitive creatures are less prone to disease. With complexity comes vulnerability.

The Caddy lover next door told her that things were heating up and she should be careful about going out. An old woman had been attacked at a nearby supermarket when she bumped her cart into a testy young woman in the check-out line. "Get the hell back," the woman shouted at her. "You don't keep your ten feet I'm gonna smack your head open." Immediately, she cracked a coconut over the woman's head. "Old gal died right there on the spot," the Caddy lover said. "Right there in the store. That's cold. But you know it's gonna happen, 'cause when people get scared they get crazy."

Macy didn't want to believe this. By and large, people seemed rational enough to her. Some made outrageous claims on social media, but these were outrageous times. People were trying to make sense of them. As she stood on the sidewalk talking to the Caddy lover, a tanker truck came by spraying the street with a pungent disinfectant. Macy had to retreat into her yard to avoid being sprayed. "What's the point of spraying the street, man?" the Caddy lover shouted. "You need to spray the air." But Macy understood that fear demands action, even when that action won't make any difference. People spray down sidewalks with hoses, some crowd together in church, some smack people with coconuts, some sing to the night sky. Whatever helps—even when it doesn't. She herself was writing a novel and was convinced that The Woman On The Corner had been sucked into its pages. She'd fled to the island. This would explain why no one had seen her.

On her walk that afternoon, two boys sped toward Macy on skateboards. She thought they would veer off the sidewalk onto the street when they got close. But they didn't. She realized at the last moment that they planned to pass very close to her or possibly hit her and fled up onto a lawn and fell to her knees. As he passed, one of the boys leered back at her with a gargoyle's grin that froze her heart. The boys stopped, and she feared they would come back. They seemed to discuss it, then went on, grinning lewdly back at her. What was happening to the world? When she was growing up, children respected adults. But maybe it went beyond disrespect. People said that some who were seemingly oblivious or distracted by their cell phones as they passed too close to you in public were in truth clandestine carriers, undercover so to speak, hoping to catch victims off guard and breathe on them. They came in many guises: a jogger who veered toward her as if to chase her down when she fled the sidewalk into the street, an old woman with a cane at the grocery store who came right up behind her, gasping for air and coughing, tapping her cane imperatively on the floor. Macy was sure she was infected. She thought to call security but hated making a fuss. Always had. Now it seemed even children were Foul Air sneak thieves. She didn't wish to believe children capable of such a thing, but likely once they were infected they were no longer children but had become hybrid monsters: human on the outside, fibrous on the inside.

A doctor in Venezuela, who dissected a suspected Hunter found dead in a gutter, reported that his lungs, heart, and veins were all clogged with a fibrous substance hard as concrete but resembling intricate spider webs. A person couldn't survive in such a state, and he hadn't. But how long did they live before they were too clogged with fibers to continue? No one knew. Since their corpses were so rarely found, it was impossible for scientists to study them. When rarely they did, they themselves were certain to become bloated with FAS and disappear soon thereafter. Only the bravest doctors and nurses would enter hospitals anymore since nearly 50% of those who did died within weeks. The question was: Where did they go? What became of the infected? Did they gather in caves, as a Hindu anchorite in India claimed? He lived in a cave himself before they evicted him. Surely in such caves they became familiar with bats, cohabiting with them, and those creatures flew out into the night to infect others. Those few in the neighborhood who ventured out at night reported seeing hundreds of bats swarming like moths around street lights. Even creepier was the unnatural silence of the city. No traffic passed along Jefferson, no planes flew overhead. Los Angeles was dead quiet, the streets deserted. At another time, this might have been marvelous, but those who ventured out found it chilling and reported seeing solitary Hunters passing at a distance, stopping to sniff the air.

Willy and Jackal spent the remainder of the day after their confrontation with the creature in the kitchen and rear bedroom of the small house. Willy assured his restless dog, "We can handle this a few days, Jacko. I could put you out back, but I can't be sure that thing won't jump the fence."

This would have sounded preposterous to him a few hours earlier, before he'd gotten a good look at the beast. It had long thin limbs and stringy muscles and reminded him of a grasshopper.

They were running out of food and toilet paper, no kibble left for Jackal. Willy had intended to get out to the store that afternoon, but the creature was blocking access to his car. He hated going shopping, having to dodge away from people who approached too close down an aisle or crowded in on you at the check-out counter. "Back off," he barked. "I'm not kidding, my man. I have an anger management issue." He wore Luella's scarf as a face mask and constantly cleared his throat to keep other shoppers away; even thought of wearing a sign around his neck: INFECTED.

Perhaps the creature was no longer on the porch. Willy didn't dare look through the front door peephole to find out since it required going into the living room, which he didn't dare do until the Foul Air cleared. He took the step-ladder out of the garage to look over the high steel gate that permitted access to the backyard via a driveway running beside the house. He saw his car parked in the drive near the street undisturbed, but no sign of the intruder. Of course, he couldn't see him on the porch from that vantage. He thought to throw a rock to draw the creature out. But that would alert it that he was in the backyard, which might not be wise.

Another idea occurred to him: he could climb over the fence, let himself quietly down the other side, and sprint for the car, leap into it and speed away. If the creature was snoozing or caught off guard he might just make it. Or the trespasser might even be on the far side of the house checking to see if it could pry open a window. If so, the neighbors would surely call Willy to warn him that there was a prowler on his property. Actually, he might give them a call to see if they'd seen anything. Or call Hicks whose tidy backyard he could see from his perch on the ladder. Maybe Hicks would be willing to step outside and look over from his front yard to see if there was anyone on the porch. Surely he would be willing to do so since Hicks didn't much believe in this Foul Air business. Willy would tell him he thought there was a homeless man on his porch, a nasty-looking sort; he didn't want to confront him. But he didn't want to put Hicks in harm's way if this truly was a Hunter. Trouble doesn't go away just because you don't believe in it. But maybe this particular Hunter had his sights set on Willy, and Hicks wouldn't interest him. Maybe they had assignments. He'd heard an expert in Washington say that each of the "Foul-Air hosts" passes FAS on to two or three people on average. Surely, they were selective about their victims.

Whoever had gone after The Woman On The Corner probably lived nearby. It wouldn't surprise him if it was one of her neighbors who threw the block party, since they were at loggerheads, and some of them had surely been infected. But the most likely candidate was Taylor; he despised the woman. But when Willy saw him on his morning walk some days back, Taylor looked healthy and expressed concern about The Woman. "I ain't seen her in a week. Usually, she be coming outside several times a day to throw me a dirty look." He was genuinely upset. Remarkable, Willy thought, the impact trouble has on people. Some collapse under its weight. Some find their worst selves in a crisis. Others, like Taylor, find their best. He would like to count himself among their number but given his ugly reaction to the man on his front porch it didn't seem he was.

It troubled him to realize that the creature didn't have to remain confined to the porch; it could be lurking most anywhere. Waiting on the other side of the gate the next time Willy looked over, it could leap up and seize his arm. A disturbing notion, as was the realization that they would be out of food tomorrow. He could go over the back fence, but would have to cut through the razor wire to get over, then navigate past the rear neighbor's dog. Mr. Hokaiddo had lived in the house behind his for decades and Willy knew him well. They exchanged oranges and persimmons over the back fence before he died. Recently, a young White couple, whom he didn't know, had moved into the house behind him and installed the razor wire. Surely, they would think him a thief or a Hunter if he suddenly appeared in their backyard. They might be armed.

He could call Hicks or the neighbor on the other side and ask if they would buy a few groceries for him and hand them over the back fence. He would offer to barbecue them a steak for their trouble once the crisis had passed. But they would think it odd that he wanted his groceries handed over the fence rather than brought to the front door. What reason could he give them? That his front door was jammed and he couldn't get out to the car? Or that he feared the front porch was infected with Foul Air? This was, of course, true. No, he didn't want to burden them. Everyone was afraid to go shopping since grocery stores ranked second among the worst Foul Air zones. Their shelves were half empty anyway. There were stories of shoppers fighting over air freshener and insecticide sprays that were said to drive away Foul Air carriers. People fought over soap and mouthwash. A man planted a buck knife in the back of another shopper in Chicago when both reached for the last package of ground beef in the cooler at the same moment. The security man wouldn't go near the killer and no one called the police, so the fellow literally got away with murder.

He could call Macy. She wouldn't think it odd that he wanted his groceries handed over a neighbor's fence. She knew he was quirky and spoke regularly to his dead wife on the front porch. She knew he became sucked into worlds he found inside books and could remain in them for days. She would likely think he had just reread *The Count of Monte Cristo* and thought he was trapped in a prison cell, as he essentially was. She would play along. But he didn't want to burden her with it either. They would just have to get by on whatever scraps he could find in the cupboards.

THOMAS SANCHEZ COULDN'T BE CERTAIN he saw The Woman On The Corner when he went out to his porch just before dawn one morning, but he knew someone was watching him. He loved the peace and quiet at that hour: no one stirring in the neighborhood. It reminded him of his youth in San Antonio. Those were different times. People were more hopeful back then, even in his dirt-poor neighborhood. They didn't believe that things would get worse, as people did now, but that they would get better. He believed people back then would have collectively willed the Foul Air away; they wouldn't have accepted it. Landlords wouldn't have evicted tenants who fell behind on their rent because they couldn't go to work. The government wouldn't have to order them to provide rent relief; they would have done it on their own. If officials did order it, landlords would have complied without complaint. Now he heard reports that people in the neighborhood were being evicted when they fell a few days behind on rent. Bloodsucking landlords sent thugs to throw their belongings out on the street. Where did they expect them to go? Tens of thousands would become homeless, forced to live in crowded camps inundated with Foul Air. People had no compassion anymore. FAS had nothing to do with Bad Air, rather God had breathed his judgment down on an immoral people like he'd once destroyed Sodom and Gomorrah.

Thomas saw what many would have called a Hunter slinking along the street. From the back, he looked a lot like Hicks who lived next door to Willy Jefferson. His graying, disheveled hair gave him away more than the black hoodie, since everyone wore black hoodies. Hicks had a variety of them, sporting odd slogans across the chest: "IF I'M SECOND, WHO'S FIRST?" or "GIVE ME LIBERTY OR GIVE ME ICE CREAM." Surely, these so-called "carriers" or "Hunters" seen wandering the streets were just people like Hicks who were going stir crazy and needed to get out for a walk.

Then he saw her for sure: a small oval face peek-a-boo-ing over a low fence that bordered his lot on the north side. Her face would pop up for a look at him then disappear. Why didn't she show herself? The fourth time she popped up, he realized for certain that it was The Woman On The Corner. He stood up. "Are you all right? We've been worried about you; there's been rumors. You shouldn't be sneaking about like that. It makes people nervous."

The final time she popped up, her face was hazy, as if covered with silk netting. Spooky. Then she was gone. Perhaps two minutes later, Macy appeared around the corner. "You're out early," he called to her. "Whazzup?"

"I've been writing all night and needed some air. Wheewy. At this rate, I'll finish my novel by the end of the week."

He grinned at her. "Superwoman. The Woman On The Corner was just here. You must've passed her."

"I didn't see her. I haven't for a while. No one is out except the two of us."

"You must have. She was headed your direction just a minute ago. She couldn't have vanished."

"People do, you know. Lots of them." She was tempted to tell him she thought The Woman On The Corner had entered her novel but thought better of it. "Things are odd now. You can't trust your own senses. That crow came pecking at my window again last night. I saw it plain as day, but I don't believe it was actually there. My mind was playing tricks on me."

"I just saw Hicks plain as day," Thomas said. "Not many of us out, but there's a few."

"I heard Mr. Hicks is ill. But you can't be sure what's true anymore. So many rumors."

"There will be rumors and rumors of rumors," he said. Macy thought it quaint that he was always inventing Biblical passages that sounded authentic but weren't gospel. He had a knack for it. She might suggest that he rewrite the Good Book using his own phraseology if she didn't think it would offend him. Like her, he'd missed his true calling.

"I've got to go," she said. "This is my chance to get to the store early enough that there might be something left on the shelves, although I'm exhausted. I understand why stores are out of Kleenex and salt; people think gargling with salt protects them from Foul Air. But why are they hoarding eggs and coconuts?"

"Toilet paper," he said, "and vinegar. It smells of apple cider vinegar everywhere you go these days. People keep it simmering on the stove. They claim it drives out the Foul Air. Another old wives' tale. The neighborhood reeks of it."

On her walk yesterday, Macy had passed the Caddy Lover washing his car down with a strong vinegar solution. "I wish I'd discovered this stuff years ago," he told her. "It buffs up beautiful."

When she returned home there was a message from Willy Jefferson. "I have a...well, call it a favor to ask of you, Macy... you know, reluctantly. Just say no if you don't want to.... you understand? Don't be bashful....Hey, I know...I don't want you to do anything that makes you...you know, uncomfortable...Okay? I won't do that...alright? Don't hesitate... promise me! Hey, Jackal—" he shouted "—get your ass outta there! I apologize; he's upset. That's why I'm calling...you understand? No, no...come to think of it....You know what, forget about it....Don't worry about it. I'll figure something else out." He hung up.

She had no idea what he was talking about and apparently he didn't either. She would stop by his place after shopping to check up on him. This was a time when people needed to look out for each other.

WILLY DECIDED IT WAS TIME TO BREAK curfew and enter the living room. He needed to see if the intruder was still there. No other way to find out. Besides, Jackal had been in several times to sniff at the door and didn't seem any the worse for it. The first couple of times he growled low in his throat and sniffed furiously under the door, vacuuming in whatever scent his olfactory intelligence was trying to process, then began whining. Like he couldn't decide whether the intruder was friend or foe.

Willy saw through the peephole that the ogre was still seated on the plastic lawn chair as he had been for the past 72 hours. Willy's heart pounded and he labored to breathe, momentarily afraid the creature had infected him with Foul Air when it charged the front door. He shoved the fear away as he'd learned to do with his PTSD attacks. He was just aggrieved that the creature wasn't gone, having an anxiety attack. This had become more than just an inconvenience. It was a serious threat.

He quietly opened the door to get a better look at him through the screen door and was startled to see a crow, likely the very bird that had attacked him, perched on the intruder's shoulder. Its head swiveled to study him with those cold black BB eyes, as did the creature's, like their brains were connected. No doubt of it: they were working as a team. Likely the Hunter rumors were true and true that crows hunted with them. They were the Hunters' hounds. The bird had surely communicated to the ogre what Willy had been up to: how he stood studying the back fence and took a ladder out to peer into the rear neighbor's yard, plotting escape, and looked over the front gate at his car, thinking of making a dash for it. If he tried, Willy realized, the creature would tackle him. They were an evil team. No doubt about it. It's why there was an influx of crows. Hunters used them as scouts. And something more. They were undertakers.

Carrion crows are scavengers known to feed on corpses. Perhaps they had made a pact with the Hunters. They followed them out to barren places after Hunters had infected their victims and waited for them to die, then feasted on them. This would explain why so few bodies were found. Though somewhere there must be piles of clean white bones. It also explained why the crows were so sleek and fat. A demonic alliance. The crows received nourishment, but what did the Hunters get in return? Doubtless, the arrangement helped propagate their species. For, in essence, Hunters became another species after they were infected with Foul Air, a species whose sole purpose was to perpetuate its kind—like a virus. Willy couldn't fully work it out since he had a limited understanding of genetics. A Hunter infected two or three victims, and the Foul Air it carried invaded organs of its victims—the new hosts—after which the Hunter died and its portion of Foul Air died with it, just as viruses die when their hosts die. But a portion of Foul Air survived in the new hosts and fed on them. So Hunters needed to constantly infect others to keep their species going. By serving as intermediaries, crows helped spread the ailment to others. More importantly, they helped Hunters stalk their prey. A scheme of brilliant, if diabolical, interspecies cooperation. People noted increasing numbers of crows. They were thriving under the scheme, dining on their allies.

Studying this baleful duo, his fear replaced by curiosity, Willy realized with a shock that the intruder was his neighbor Hicks.

He hadn't recognized him previously, given his grotesquely wrinkled skin and blue-green hue, eyes sunk deep in his skull. Poor fellow did not look at all well but ill in every conceivable way: mentally, morally, physically, and—Thomas Sanchez would say—spiritually. Hideously transformed. All the insurance in the world couldn't help him now. It was quite a shock. The bird leapt off Hicks' shoulder with a great flapping of wings, skimmed past the door, just missing Willy's nose, and flew off. Gone hunting no doubt. Surely, they had selected him as a victim, but needed at least one more to insure the survival of the species. Maybe Yolanda up the block, who was always on Hicks about the length of his grass. But why had Hicks chosen him? The man had always seemed to admire him, inquiring, "What language you studying now, Willy? I've never been any good at languages." Maybe simply because he lived next door. As baleful as the Foul Air infection was, there was no reason to assume Hunters were baleful. Just helping to perpetuate their species like any other organism.

Hicks seemed suddenly very human to him—his familiar neighbor whose hair was always mussed as if he'd just gotten out of bed—certainly no alien. Poor man struggled to breathe and sweated profusely, shivering nonstop at times, teeth chattering furiously. "You don't look so good, Hicks," he said. "You want me to call 9-1-1 or your wife?" Yes, what had become of his wife? Had Hicks infected her and sent her out looking for her own victims? Likely this happened all the time: couples that had once had children together conspired to help perpetuate their new species. Hicks turned to look at him for a time, weakly reaching out a hand, seeming to want to speak. "What is it, Hicks?" If he spoke, even subliminally, Willy couldn't hear him. The poor man kept working his mouth as if it was dry. How long since he'd had a sip of water or anything to eat? He had that famished look Hunters were said to have. What was his duty here, Willy wondered. After all, he knew the man.

"Sure, I'm shit scared of him," he told Luella quietly, "the way he looks and all. I know he's deadly dangerous. But he's a fellow human. He's our neighbor. I can't just stand here watching the poor bastard suffer. Even Jacko seems to wonder what to do. You see how he approaches the door, whining, then backs off like he's spooked. Should I bring the man a glass of water? It's the least I can do. What d'you think? Maybe a blanket? Poor bastard is shivering with fever. Maybe splash him down with cold water, like how you brought my fever down that time I had pneumonia. Bring him a couple Tylenol. Risky, yeah, but wouldn't I want him to do the same for me? Do unto others and all. That's what you'd advise me."

At that instant, as if in answer to his quandary, he saw air distort around Hicks like a gossamer shroud had fallen over him, causing his face to blur. He'd never seen anything like it. It occurred to Willy that very few people had observed a Hunter close up and survived to tell about it. He had a duty to take pictures of the man on his iPhone and post them on the Internet. Tell the world what he observed in low tones so as not to alarm Hicks. That way, even if he didn't survive this, there would be a record. It would give the experts a better idea of what they were up against and might even help bring this horror to an end. He found opportunity to nudge the door open wide enough to snap a few pictures when the crow returned with a great flurry of wings and landed on Hicks' shoulder. It reminded Willy of Dust Offs in 'Nam and sent a shiver of horror through him. Snap, snap, snap. Gotchou! The crow mewled contentedly. No doubt of it: they were a team, those two, man and pet. Alien pals. The bird studied him with malevolent intent as did Hicks. So Willy closed the steel door and continued shooting video through the mesh. Although it was distorted, you could make out a ghostly figure with a bird perched on its shoulder, which added eeriness and mystery to the scene. He posted what he had shot on Instagram.

Peering out the large plate glass window that looked onto the street, he saw Macy O'Brien approaching along the sidewalk, clearly headed for his door given the tentative way she was looking at the house. Good God! Had the crow found some devious way to lure her here so Hicks could jump her? Had they selected her as their next victim? Willy stepped close to the window so she could see him—just out of sight of those two on the porch—and waved his arms overhead. She halted on the sidewalk with an alarmed look. He held his phone up to the window and called her.

"Are you all right, Willy?" she asked at once. "Are you ill?"

"Don't come any closer," he whispered. "No time to explain, Macy. You've got to turn around and get the hell outta here. Now. Do it, girl! Go!"

She hesitated, looking at his car, trying to see the porch, but couldn't from that vantage. "I don't see anything."

"Damn you, Macy. Don't argue. Run! It's a matter of life and death."

She did: first small, mincing steps, then a trot, finally broke into a run as panic seized her. Remarkably, the ghouls on the porch didn't see her.

Enough of this, he thought. I'll chase them the hell off for good and final. Fire a warning shot! But what if they won't go? What if it truly is Hicks? I can't shoot my neighbor in cold blood even if I think he is a monster. Who will believe me? In the main, he knew, authorities didn't buy into the Hunter hypothesis. He hadn't either until one showed up on his porch. Had The Woman On The Corner and Mrs. Hernandez experienced something similar? Seeing someone sitting on the porch or going through their garbage, as homeless people sometimes did, they'd gone out to shoo them off and had been jumped and dragged into the house like a cat might drag a mouse. Now it was his turn.

On his way to the bedroom for the gun—to have it at the ready, anyway—passing the bookshelf in the dining room, he saw a copy of Tolstoy's collected stories which contained the long story "Father Sergius," which had made quite an impression on him when he was a young man. For some inexplicable reason, given those two ghouls on the porch and no food in the house, he sat down on the couch to reread the story. The reinforced screen door was locked, but the wooden front door stood ajar, and Jackal lay with his chin on his paws keeping an eye on the intruders. Willy realized he was reading Tolstoy for advice, hoping to gain some insight into his predicament. He had thought to call his son Justin to discuss it. He would most certainly be home since he worked as a rigger in the entertainment industry which had suspended productions until the Foul Air crisis passed. But he didn't relish the prospect of talking to Justin, could nearly hear his broad laugh and Justin admonishing, "What the hell, Pop. Kick his ass the fuck off your porch. Hey, you're not going old man on me, are you?" He was looking for a different kind of advice.

Once he'd finished "Father Sergius," he read Flaubert's long story, "The Legend of Saint Julian the Hospitaller," and spent much of the afternoon reflecting on the meaning of the two stories as they applied to his current dilemma: what he should do about Hicks. The message of the stories was clear enough: It's in humble self-sacrifice that we find peace, gratification, and redemption for our own misdeeds, putting others' needs above our own even if it puts us in harm's way. Love thy neighbor. Clearly, Hicks was in great pain. Willy could hear him moaning beyond the open door: long sighing groans interspersed with coughing fits, so even at this distance Willy dared not take off his bandana. Whatever his intentions, the man certainly lacked the strength to tackle him and fill him with Foul Air. He would be grateful for whatever Willy could do for him: bring him to the table and feed him, call his wife. Yes, why hadn't he called the man's wife? What was he waiting for? Perhaps Hicks would want to lay down on the couch and rest; his back must be stiff from sitting up for so long.

"You can't worry too much about your own well-being at a time like this," he told the open door. "Times like this demand sacrifice. We must do our duty, and I know what mine is now, Hicks." He asked Luella what she thought. "I know, I know! Do the right thing. That's what you always told me. 'Do the right thing, Willy. It's simple.' You don't think Hicks wishes me any harm, do you? That damn bird maybe, but not Hicks. I'm telling you, I'll blow it out of the air if it comes in here. Hicks, fine, but not the bird. Have we got that straight?" he asked loudly enough for them to hear him.

Still, he hesitated to act. If you don't know your enemy—or even whether he truly is your enemy—you can't know what to do.

That night he studied Hicks through the peephole. The porch light bathed him in an otherworldly glow. He'd pulled the hood over his head, which was tilted forward so that his chin rested on his chest. He appeared to be sleeping, snoring so loudly that the sound penetrated the door. Less snore than deep wheezing as he struggled for breath. From time to time, his whole body shuddered as he labored to replace the Foul Air that had filled his lungs with sweet, moisture-laden night air that rolled in off the Pacific. Willy couldn't imagine what agony it must be to have your lungs fill with fibrous cement. He was suddenly flooded with pity for the man, still under the spell of those two stories that had filled him with compassion for all mankind. Very slowly and quietly, he opened the door and continued to study Hicks, assuring himself that he was asleep. The crow, too, had gone off to sleep wherever crows go. Stepping outside and silently approaching, he saw dirt caked under Hicks' fingernails; his hands were covered with black dirt as if he'd been digging a grave with them. The thought sent a chill through Willy. Whose grave? Were they required to dig their own graves? He crept forward with a bottle of water and a few crackers on a paper plate, the last food he had in the house, which he placed on the tiles at Hicks' feet. Turning to go back in the house, he heard Hicks' shoes scrape across tiles behind him. Willy fled inside and slammed the door closed.

How foolish to entertain inviting that creature into the house—to literally invite infection inside. You wished to do good, but to do certain harm to yourself to help another resulted in no gain for human well-being, which might be fine if you were a saint or it redounded to the greater good of all. But he wasn't a saint. Besides, it was doubtful that inviting Hicks in could do him any good now; he was too far gone. Beyond that, helping Hicks and almost certainly becoming infected with FAS himself would turn him into a Hunter and make him a threat to others. Under such circumstances, compassion was a curse. What a strange idea.

Jackal gave a sudden gunshot bark that jarred Willy half out of his wits and leapt toward the front window. Willy followed on tiptoe, pulling the curtain aside, expecting to see a duo of Hunters trudging along the street, heads lowered. Instead, he saw Hicks' face pressed against the glass, hideously distorted, nose broad as a pig's snout, nostrils flaring, sunken eyes reflecting lamp light from inside and beaming it back into Willy's eyes, amplifying it so it blinded him and gave him an instant headache. The man was gesturing to come inside. He looked dreadful, clearly on his last legs. "No!" Willy shouted, pulling the curtain closed. "Damn you, Jacko. You could have warned me it was him." Then he realized that he had. It occurred to him that Hicks might be nearing the point where he would have to retreat to the woods with his crow escort to die. Maybe he had outlasted them.

WHEN MACY FLED WILLY'S HOUSE, four crows followed her home. Nearing her house, she was overcome with exhaustion and couldn't pull in enough oxygen to keep her legs moving or remain upright. She collapsed and had to crawl the final fifty feet across the lawn to her front door on hands and knees, with crows pecking at the soles of her feet. She wouldn't likely have made it to the house but for fear of them. She just managed to close the door and leaned back against it, struggling to catch her breath. She had never felt so weak. It was many minutes before she stopped panting and her heart stopped pounding. Just anxiety, she thought. Willy and the crows had given her a fright. It seemed they had been expecting her arrival, perched in a row on Willy's roof. Lined up now out front on the sidewalk. Others had joined them, maybe twenty crows in all, daring her to come outside. Would they attack her in a frenzy of pecking or blow Foul Air at her? She continued struggling to breathe. Was she exhibiting the first signs of Foul Air Syndrome? The thought struck terror into her. Shortness of breath, sudden loss of her sense of smell. She realized she hadn't smelled a trace of the mordant vinegar that permeated the neighborhood as she sprinted home, nor the stench of rotting food in garbage bins she passed, which had grown fouler since they'd stopped picking up the trash a week ago and people had begun piling garbage in black bags beside the bins as they did in New York City, attracting rats. She could hear them squealing all night long. It was said The Waste Haulers Union had gone on strike and stopped collecting trash because their workers weren't being supplied with masks to protect them from Foul Air. Although some said the city had ordered them to stop collecting in hopes that Foul Air would be replaced by the putrid air that rose off rotting garbage, which was at least organically based, while Foul Air had come up from hell. She was assaulted by a splitting headache at the front of her head that blurred her vision. Her chest ached and had begun to tingle, as did her arms; she'd heard this referred to as "tingleitis," a definitive symptom of Foul Air Syndrome.

She could not imagine how or where she'd picked up the infection. She was being cautious, always wore a mask when she went out, two masks and goggles when rarely she went shopping, every inch of her body covered in plastic garbage bags. She always crossed the street when she saw someone approaching along the sidewalk. She no longer sat in the backyard. She no longer risked talking to Thomas Sanchez even from twenty feet away. He was going a bit loopy, anyway, insisting that tiny demons hid under his bed. He was burning incense inside his house to keep them at bay. She avoided walking past The Woman On The Corner's house, certain now that she lay dead inside. Even Mr. Taylor, who'd always disliked the woman, was distraught. Our world can be shaken nearly as much when things we dislike disappear from our lives as when things we like do. We are a creature of habit that thrives on the familiar, whether good or bad, and fears the unknown.

After taking a couple of Aspirin and lying for a time on the couch, she felt somewhat better and decided her symptoms were psychosomatic, caused by angst. She sat down at the desk hoping to get back into the novel to take her mind off things. It had stalled when the single-celled humans living in stagnant pools on her island rebelled and demanded their creator grant them freedom of individual expression, protesting what they called "the tyranny of sameness." They called her a fascist. Strangely, this happened just when rebellious demonstrators across the country began protesting "tyrannical" governmental actions to prevent the spread of FAS—draconian stay-at-home orders, closure of businesses and banning of public gatherings, mandating the wearing of masks—insisting on their right to become infected with Foul Air if they so wished, even inviting Hunters to join their protests. This may have happened in Cincinnati when dozens of protesters came down with FAS after one such rally. The general theme of the protests was that Foul Air Syndrome was an invention of the liberal media and its deep state allies.

The islanders in her novel insisted they needed some form of social order to protect individual liberties—laws and governing bodies, economic organization, protection from their many predators, a health care system—which was to say they needed a social hierarchy, leaders and followers. Her original conception was slipping away as they took control of their story, threatening to devolve back to humans again. They said it was their destiny; humans would always be humans. "That defeats the whole purpose of my novel," she protested. "I wouldn't have written it if I knew you were going to sabotage my vision." She realized she could do nothing to prevent it. After all, it was their story. They had a right to choose their own destiny. How often, she wondered, did writers encounter such rebellion, having their plans sabotaged by their own characters, their attempt to play God foiled.

Beyond this, she realized that a novel, like a human life, must come to an end. It is finite. This was depressing, especially now when the world itself seemed to be ending. She had hoped her novel might resist that.

Instead of working on the novel, she looked up the writer across town who was writing *The Great Unseen* and found his email address. She wrote him a note telling him about her novel and asking if he might have any suggestions about how to end it. "I have taught literature long enough to know novels must have a climax, but how do you recognize a climax when it arrives? Does the climax dictate the ending? One last question, forgive me for asking: Is it possible to forego an ending altogether? Oh, and yes, do your characters ever rebel and take control of your books?" The moment she hit the send button she knew he wouldn't reply.

Then she began coughing nonstop: a dry, hacking, insidious cough which seemed desperate to expel something that would not leave her lungs. Her chest was heavy and she was feverish. She thought to call 9-1-1, but it was said that hospitals were death traps and many medical personnel, especially EMTs, were infected with Foul Air, so most patients disappeared before even reaching the hospital. It wasn't known what happened to those who were hospitalized since only the ill were permitted inside hospitals. They simply vanished. You were better off riding out the Bad Air at home, hoping you were one of the lucky few who had developed some resistance. "Herd immunity" it was called.

Perhaps this was how her novel would end: muck ponds on the island would dry up once global warming brought endless drought to the island, and the human amoeba would die off. She could hear their tiny, shrieking bacterial cries as they perished. The house echoed with them. A carpet of green slime mold crawled under her and began to ferry her across the living room floor. She realized that she had set this horror loose on the world. It had crawled out of her novel just as The Woman On The Corner had crawled in. She understood vaguely that she was hallucinating. It was said that FAS victims often did. The crows were not really chanting her name in unison like supporters at a political rally.

She thought to call Willy Jefferson to let him know that she might be infected with Foul Air, so someone knew. She had no significant other or children, her parents were dead, she had no siblings, she'd lost contact with all her old friends, her colleagues at the university were mostly too self-absorbed to be friendly with each other. She might call her chair or the student who took control of her class on Macy's off days, but she didn't have the girl's number. Willy made the most sense. He was in a similar position, although he had a son. But she knew he had his own troubles and hesitated to add to them. She must summon all her strength just to pick up the phone and was scarcely able to speak.

Somehow she managed to crawl to a window and pry it open, desperate for air. Crows hopped closer and formed a semi-circle under the window, cawing at her. Then, incredibly, an ambulance arrived. She hadn't summoned it. Two young EMTs in shiny space suits, wearing masks, goggles, and hairnets, hurried toward the house with a stretcher. Another hallucination? She couldn't be sure, not even when their heads popped and released puffs of brown air. Those days anything was possible.

WILLY HAD DECIDED TO CALL his son Justin. He and Jackal had nothing to eat the day before but stale saltine crackers and oatmeal that tasted moldy, to which he could add neither milk nor sugar since he had none; he doused it with salt to make it more palatable for Jackal, but the dog turned up his nose, preferring to starve than to eat the insipid mush. Willy saw the date on the oatmeal container: *best by April 4, 2006*—twenty years ago. Damn! He really must call Justin and ask him to bring groceries, most anything, before they starved or poisoned themselves. Surely Hicks was weak enough by now that Justin could safely get past him or could run down the drive to the back gate and hand grocery bags over it to his father.

Willy told his son that Hicks had been sitting in his chair on the front porch for four days. "I believe the man is sick. He sure as hell looks sick."

"Why are you whispering, Pop?"

"You'd whisper too if you saw him. Sometimes a crow sits on his shoulder. They're a Foul Air Syndrome tag team. I think they've singled me out."

"Damn, Pop!" Justin made a whooshing sound with his mouth and said much what Willy expected him to say: "Chase them the fuck off. A crow? Damn! Whassup with that, man? Usually you'd be on it. You ain't goin' old man on me now are you?"

"Check my latest Instagram posts. You'll see what I'm talking about. This isn't your typical trespassing dickhead. You'll see. The man is a fiend. I thought I better photograph him since nobody hardly has seen one up close and lived to tell about it. I'm surprised no one has reacted yet. I thought my post would go viral."

Willy could hear Justin fumbling with his phone. He could do three or four tasks on it at once, a skill he himself had not mastered. "Got it, Pop." He guffawed. "Who's gonna react to that, man? Pics of your funky old chair and a lame video of the screen door? Damn! You whispering about a Hunter's on your porch and shit. I mean, what the hell's that? I'd take it down if I was you, Pop. Makes you look like a dumb ass."

"You saying you don't see him? The Hunter or whatever the hell they are sitting right there in my chair? Hicks and his pet crow sitting on my porch? You don't see them?"

"Ain't nothing there, Pop. Just the fuckin' chair. What about Hicks? I've known the man my whole life. Ain't nothin' wrong with him sitting on the porch."

Willy ran into the den and brought the post up on his laptop. "He's there plain as day. I'm looking at him right now. Better shots than I thought I got, too. His lips look smarmy and—what's it called?—cyanotic. Turning blue. Plain as day."

"What you smoking, Pop?" Justin laughed.

"You'll see. Come over and you'll see. He's out there right now. Listen, son, I need you to buy me some groceries since I can't get out. All right? There's nothing in the house. Jacko needs dog food. Give me a call when you pull up. You can run down the drive and hand it over the gate to me. Likely, he'll be asleep and won't even see you, but be careful."

"What the fuck, Pop? You're really serious about this."

An hour later, Willy was surprised to hear the doorbell ring and Justin calling to him through the door. Had he lost his mind, sharing that tiny space with Hicks and his bird? He threw the door open so Justin could get inside out of danger, slammed and leaned back against it once he'd come in. "What the hell's the matter with you? I warned you to stay off the porch. You young people aren't immune to this even if you think you're invincible. Same as I did at your age. 'Nam taught me different. You saw the man; you saw how sick he is."

"I didn't see shit, Pop. Just like I thought. No one's fuckin' there." His son shook his head in a dismissive why-am-I-wasting-my-time-even-talking-to-you gesture, much like his mother used to do.

Willy was stunned. He cautiously opened the door again to look. Hicks was there all right, but not as substantial as he'd been just hours before, significantly blurred and wraith-like. One half of his face was clearly Hicks, the other half molten flesh that threatened to drip off his chin. The outline of his body clear enough but empty inside. Hollow. "What happened to him?" he asked. "The thing hollowed him out. I'm telling you he's there, son, as real as you or me...almost."

Justin regarded him with a look more concerned than puzzled now. "Listen, Pop, you been having memory troubles, right? Losing your car keys and shit. Right? Leaving the gas ring on? You remember what happened to Big Papa: Alzheimer's and shit. You ain't goin' brain dead on me, are you, old man?"

"Isn't nothing wrong with my brain."

Justin opened the door to get the sacks of groceries he'd left on the porch. "See! Ain't nobody there."

For a moment it was true: Hicks had vanished. And the bird. But when Justin began to sit down in the chair to prove it was empty, Willy grabbed his arm and yanked him away. "Are you crazy? Listen, that chair's contaminated with whatever residue they leave behind. You understand? It's gotta be sterilized. I'll likely throw it out." Jackal had come out to inspect the chair, smelling every inch, not growling or mewling, so it must have been empty for him too. Willy was baffled. Was the anxiety of the moment playing tricks on his mind? He'd heard of that happening. "FAS trauma," they called it, something like PTSD. Some said this whole Foul Air panic was nothing but group hysteria. However, Jackal sniffed and smelled the chair obsessively, proof that something had been sitting in it.

Willy agreed to go shopping with his son, since he would need more than two small bags of groceries to last the month, although he was reluctant to get in the car with him, wore his face mask and hugged the passenger-side door. Justin shook his head. "What the hell, Pop? You think I'm contaminated? Damn!"

"You just about sat in it. Foul air was pooled all around you; I saw it. Hell yes you could be contaminated. Or I could. I've had enough exposure. The thing is, we don't know. Nobody knows. That's the problem. You can't trust yourself or nobody else either. That's the curse of this thing. You'd get through it fine, but it would likely kill me."

When they got back to the house, Justin walked him inside. Although Willy couldn't see Hicks, he gave the chair wide berth, suspecting it was one of their devious tricks, some arrangement they had made with the air to conceal themselves inside it when they didn't wish to be seen. It didn't mean they weren't there. The phone rang soon after Justin left. Willy thought he was calling to say he'd caught a glimpse of Hicks hiding in the bushes as he drove away. The man had fled the porch to avoid Justin, since he'd come for the father not the son.

"Yes, who's calling?" Willy repeated. "Hello...anybody there?" Nobody was on the other end. Finally, he heard a tiny voice, scarcely a whisper.

"It's Macy O'Brien." She began coughing: that horrible dry, incessant hack you heard about.

"I'll call 9-1-1," Willy said. "You need to get to the hospital, Macy."

"No, no, please," she managed. "Please, Willy, no hospital."

"It's all rot and nonsense, the hospital rumors," he insisted. "You need help. A time like this, you need to trust people."

"She may be hard to deal with," he told the 9-1-1 dispatcher when he called.

"We're used to that," she told him. "All our first responders are."

He couldn't imagine doing their job, fighting off Hunters who tried to tackle them, tying victims to gurneys, working fourteen hour shifts seven days a week, hot and sweaty in hazmat suits, swimming in Foul Air that filled hospital cubicles and crept under their masks, exhausted, nerve-worn, watching the occasional carrier break loose and pin a health care worker to the floor and blow contaminated air into her mouth. It was heartbreaking work that wrung the marrow out of health care workers, taxing them to the limit. It took courage. Some would say lunacy.

He hesitated to open the door again to check Hicks' status, hoping against hope that he wouldn't be there. Perhaps never had been. He was, but fainter now, less substantial if that was possible, nearly transparent, half melted into the air. He wasn't struggling so much to breathe and was less threatening now, more like Hicks himself. His chin rested on his chest and he seemed to be asleep. Something significant was happening. Something profound. Not that the man was recovering. Rather dispersing. Disappearing to wherever they disappeared. At that moment, the crow flew onto the porch and made to land on Hicks' shoulder on a downdraft of flapping wings, but veered away as if repulsed by him. It circled the porch and fled.

Yes, something had changed.

Willy considered inviting Hicks into the house to sit in his armchair and have a beer with him, like old times. But feared he would see liquid trickling down into his stomach, transparent as he was. He stood holding the door open, wondering why Hicks wouldn't look at him. Jackal charged past and leapt for Hicks with a vicious snarl. Passed right through him—tore through more like—releasing a yellow cloud into the air. Willy retreated into the house to avoid it, but realized that Jackal was loose and headed down the street for the dog on the corner, who was his long-standing enemy. Willy charged out past Hicks and chased Jackal down the block, shouting at him to stop, which he finally did at the corner, sniffing furiously at the fence. No sign of the other dog. Willy seized Jackal's collar and walked him home, nervous about being so close to his dog, who had surely absorbed much of Hicks' toxic air when he went through him.

Reaching home, Willy realized he had left the front door standing open. Hicks wasn't on the porch. Nowhere to be seen. "Damn!" Willy cautiously entered the house, holding Jackal's collar, and fought back dread such as he hadn't felt since the jungles of Vietnam, sensing a presence in the small house. Jackal's hackles stood up; he growled and moaned, undecided between fear and fury. Hicks was hiding somewhere, prepared to jump them. A trace of his foul, catarrhal breath lingered on the air.

SHE WAS STARING UP AT STRANGE BEINGS with plastic shields over their faces who stared back at her. Actually, they had no faces. Squinty eyes peered down above pig-snout gas masks from which tubes led to tanks on their backs. They were covered head to toe in white Kevlar space suits, human in form, but they didn't act or move like humans. No doubt they were the automaton aliens who snatched people away after they were infected with Foul Air. Not Hunters but the disposal crew. Their eyes looked frightened—of her, Macy realized, and the air that she struggled to exhale. She was feverish, shivering nonstop. She could see they wanted to flee, but duty prohibited it. She counted the fingers on their rubber hands: five, so they were at least humanoid. They avoided eye contact. When she asked where she was, they clamped an oxygen mask over her mouth. So this is what it's like to die, she thought. No one speaks to you or looks at you. No one wants to look death in the eye. A woman stood in the doorway with a clipboard; she spoke briefly with the aliens and jotted something down. An actual human, Macy knew, wearing a cloth mask. She heard a whirring sound, and her lungs expanded with air as if they were balloons.

While across town, Willy and Jackal crept from room to room looking for Hicks, dodged around corners, prepared for him to leap out. When Willy reached the bedroom and flipped on the light switch, he was horrified to see Hicks stretched out on his bed, asleep or dead. The next moment he was gone, the bed untouched. Willy sank to his knees in relief. But how could he be sure? They were there and then they weren't. Some saw them and some didn't. You might be one of them and you might not be. Maybe it was himself he'd seen lying on the bed and only imagined it was Hicks.

To be safe, he quarantined Jackal in his pen in back, knowing he was contaminated with Foul Air after crashing through the creature's body. He held him off with a broom when he placed bowls of kibble and water in his pen. The poor dog whined and regarded him with bewildered eyes. "I'm not angry at you, Jacko. Just being careful. I'll let you out in a couple weeks." What an awful time: people not only fearing one another and themselves but fearing their pets. No one trusted anyone. Would that be the lasting legacy of this horror?

Maybe a week went by, maybe longer. Macy couldn't be sure. The faceless masks remained overhead. Perhaps this was what the afterlife was like: nothing ever changed, everything froze in time like something Kafka had contrived. Eternal misery, but dulled so you couldn't be sure it was real.

Willy hadn't seen Hicks since he'd found him lying on the bed. He slept on the couch in the living room just in case the man remained in the bedroom, hidden somehow in folds of air.

It had been two weeks since his last exposure to Hicks, and Willy concluded that his neighbor hadn't infected him with Foul Air since he remained symptom-free. So did Jackal, whom he let out of quarantine. Possibly little Foul Air remained in his system while Hicks sat on the front porch or the toxicity of the air had diminished. People everywhere spoke of such weakening, but he considered this wishful thinking. Although more cars were parked on the street now and more people were out walking their dogs.

He called Macy repeatedly but got no answer and feared the worst. What a pity. She was not only a fine person but the only one in the neighborhood he could talk books with. Where had she gone? Thomas Sanchez said he'd seen an ambulance come for her and saw them wheel her out on a gurney, a crow perched on her chest. Such a pity that she should be among the victims.

It was now said that the bodies of Foul Air victims who became Hunters didn't pile up in forests where crows cleaned their bones, but that they were stored in huge refrigerator trucks parked in front of hospitals or hidden away in parking lots of empty sports venues. Willy thought this ridiculous until a refrigerator truck parked on his block down near Jefferson. He heard the engine idling all night to keep the corpses cold. It made him nervous to have a truck full of them so close. But then he'd had one sitting on his porch for days. What did they plan to do with the bodies? They couldn't bury them and contaminate the earth or cremate them and poison the air. Either they would have to keep them permanently frozen or send them into space. Ferrying them to Greenland was out of the question since the ice caps were melting and would soon release the contaminated bodies into the sea.

When Willy went out walking, people were noticeably cheerier. Many no longer wore masks. He himself, after sterilizing the chair Hicks had been sitting in and putting it out in the sun for a few days, sat reading on the porch again, keeping an eye out in case Hicks sneaked up on him. Or that maniac crow. People noted there were fewer crows around. When Willy saw one approach the porch one morning, likely that devil bird, he leapt up and clapped his hands. It veered away with fearful squawks. A couple of young dudes passing by on the street clapped with him. One shouted, "Fly away, dumb ass."

When he went to volunteer at the food bank, the place was slammed. Cars and people on foot were lined up for blocks to pick up free bags of groceries. Many remained out of work and economists said it could be months before the economy picked up again; some said it never would. Dozens of people unloaded food from trucks and gathered around tables packing it into paper bags; others distributed it to the needy. Some wore masks, some didn't. The atmosphere was upbeat and cheerful. All chatted merrily and laughed. Willy realized it had been months since he'd heard laughter. "One day volunteers just started showing up. I have no idea why," the priest who ran the program told him. "Some have guilt fever like you, ashamed of doing well when so many are ill. Some have become sick of the whole thing and are willing it away. We can do that, you know, humans can. When we all decide that we must act, we can accomplish great things together. Miracles."

People told Willy they still had no work, but there were rumors of businesses starting to hire again, so that, although hungry and broke, they were no longer afraid. There was hope in the air. They said the good air was building up like a high pressure system and driving Foul Air out, pushing it high into the stratosphere where it was destroyed by ultraviolet light. People noticed it was sunnier. "Some says people pass resistance one to another," old John, who looked like an aging hippy, said. "Some says people got fed up and stood up to it. Some says it's already passed through more people than anybody knew and they got too much good air in them now to allow Bad Air in. Maybe you already had it and so did I and didn't none of us know it." Opening his arms to encompass the crowd. Yes, Willy thought, I likely caught it from Hicks, recalling the night he'd struggled to breathe and felt feverish. He dreamed vividly that night of inviting Hicks into the house and having a few beers with him, no longer fearing the man, who seemed almost normal again, his face no longer bifurcated. Jackal went to lie at his feet. When Willy woke up he felt fine.

Yes, he'd no doubt willed Hicks away—that monster anyhow that had taken hold of him. It was happening all over the neighborhood, the city, the state, the world. Everyone rising up in common cause to shoo the Three Devils away. Maybe it was the human spirit, as the priest claimed, the collective will to survive. With any luck, people might hold onto that. There were other threats on the horizon. Foul Air was just a hint of things to come.

Things were returning to normal, perhaps due to the millions of people—beginning in Italy, spreading to Spain, north through Germany, east through Russia, then to China, across the Pacific to the Americas—who stood facing the closest ocean and blowing in unison to push Foul Air off the continents. They stood on the street, on their balconies, in backyards and parks—seven billion people—all blowing at once, pushing Foul Air out to sea. The most remarkable act of human unity in history, which suggested that people could cooperate if it was in everyone's interest to do so. Men in the space station, which was said to be the safest place a human could be, felt the current of air gently rocking their craft. Willy stood out in the yard one night with others in the neighborhood, beating on an aluminum garbage can lid with a hammer, while his neighbors honked car horns, shouted, and shot off firecrackers, making a god-awful racket to chase Foul Air out of L.A. It was a joyous act of solidarity.

AS HE SAT READING ONE MORNING, Macy passed by on the street, calling to him. "Hello, Willy. So good to see you out. When Willy Jefferson is sitting on his porch reading, I know the world is returning to normal again. It makes me happy. How's Luella?"

He stood up, dumbfounded to see her. "I thought," he said, "well...my God...I thought, Macy....They took you away, and I thought, you know, how none of them come back. I thought we lost you."

"It was a horrible time," she said, "just awful. However, I scarcely recall it. Like stitches were taken in my brain and the memory sewn up. I recall odd, armored beings standing over me, automatons except for their eyes, which were human and panicked. They placed a machine that looked like a huge accordion over me and stuck a tube in my mouth. I was terrified. I thought it was the engraving machine in 'In the Penal Colony.' I don't think it was a nightmare because the woman with the clipboard came in one morning and opened the blinds and bright sunlight poured into the room. 'You can go,' she said matter of factly. 'I can see from your face that you are ready to go.'"

"So that leaves only The Woman On The Corner and Floria Hernandez we've lost in the neighborhood. Likely Hicks. Plus some people at the church."

"And the poor man who threw a party up the street, I think."

Willy shook his head. "Foolish. Seven is a tragedy for a neighborhood like ours."

"Millions," she said, "millions and millions. We'll never know how many."

Just then, to his astonishment, he saw Hicks pushing his lawnmower out to mow the front lawn. "Hicks!" he cried in surprise, not sure whether they should flee or welcome him back. But he felt emboldened and went close enough to talk over the roar of the engine. "How you feeling, my man? You all right?"

"Never better," Hicks called back. "Damn grass got too high. Time to get busy."

"The Foul Air," Willy shouted, "you breathed it out or what?"

Hicks threw a hand at him. "I never had no Bad Air. That whole business was a lot of hooey. But I'll tell you what, the insurance market is booming. People are buying it for everything. We begun offering life insurance for dogs. We can't keep up with the demand."

It was Hicks all right, back to his old self. Luella always said people were going to be who they were going to be. No changing them. "C'mon over later," Willy said, "we'll have a couple of beers and celebrate. You, too, Macy. I think we've earned it."

Just then a flock of crows flew over, cawing boisterously; the light reflecting off their glossy black feathers caused the air to shimmer and wrinkle around them.

HOW TROUBLE BEGINS

You don't always see it coming: the telltale pain in the chest that expands to angina, the stock market crash. If you are religious, you drop to your knees and beg for mercy. If an atheist, you shout curses at the elements, the Fates, your ancestors. Someone or something is to blame. We didn't arrive here by chance.

The poor woman whose antique SUV has been parked in front of my house for the past few weeks must see grief coming constantly, not just for herself but for all of us. She sits out there day and night pleading with "*El Señor*"—for what I can't be sure, since my Spanish is rusty. The way she rants and goes on, you'd think she's angry at him, or perhaps at us. Rebuking, chiding us like the Prophet Samuel—for what I'm not sure. Then you hear the agonized pleading in her voice and realize the poor woman lives in a turmoil of constant fear. Seers and prophets call it like they see it and hold nothing back. To most of us they seem mad, but what is madness anymore? Can there be madness when we are all becoming unhinged?

I work up courage to knock on the back driver's side window one day, wanting to know what she is troubled about, hoping she speaks Spanish slowly enough for me to puzzle it out. I'm curious. Moreover, I'm wondering if I might offer her some comfort: a cup of tea, navel oranges from my precious tree in back, or a blanket. She has taken up residence in front of my house so, like it or not, we are neighbors at a time when most of my neighbors have fled. I'm constantly on the verge of fleeing myself.

It appears she will not open the door, and I begin to walk away when I hear the squawk of rusted hinges behind me. A hoarse voice croaks, "What you want?" I return to the car. A wave of heat hits me from its interior like I've opened the door of the pizza oven at Sal's, where I worked as a teenager. It must be 120 degrees inside that car. Los Angeles is deceptive that way: a pleasant 93 degrees outside most days with the whisper of a breeze coming off the ocean, but inside a car with windows rolled up it's the outskirts of hell. That's why so many dogs and babies died of heat prostration in normal times, when their parents left them in the car while they ran an errand; although it was often only in the eighties back then, even in summer. By the time I was growing up in the mid-Thirties, our mean temperature was well into the nineties. A.C. was too expensive for most people to run during the few hours a day the power was on. Back then, refugees, domestic and foreign, came here in droves to escape the heat in other places, unaware that our SoCal sun blazed hotter and hotter. Less moisture in the air to filter the rays, more CO2 to trap the heat. Many were found dead in rusted old SUVs and campers, deaths we referred to as "car cooking" in L.A. speak. Not nice, but then it wasn't. Still today, mummified bodies remain in abandoned rigs on the city's wasted streets. Truth is, we are all living in a sweltering car now.

That initial heat wave is followed by a wave of nausea from the foul miasma wafting from her car. Good Lord! The smell of sewage mixed with sickly sweet cologne and body odor forces me to retreat thirty feet up onto my dirt yard, plus fear of COVID-SARSX since she isn't wearing a mask. Although it's hard to imagine any life form, human or microbial, surviving in that oven. No doubt she's a SARSX denier or believes *El Señor* will protect her. The devout often believe themselves shielded from a virus that their god released to target nonbelievers. Likely, she doesn't subscribe to the conspiracy theories circulating on the Liberty Network, claiming SARSX is a designer virus released by a deep state bio-weapons lab, much like the Coronavirus variants Chinese government labs released in the Twenties to target Western populations that eat high-carb diets—beginning with COVID-19 in 2019, the year before I was born. But such sophisticated labs surely went down in the world-wide high-tech collapse of the Forties.

One collapse led to another like a row of dominoes falling in procession—the electrical grid, big agriculture, industry, Wall Street, public institutions—exacerbated by drought, fire storms, mega-hurricanes, flooding of coastal cities, and atmospheric rivers. Western Civilization, which took millennia to build, collapsed in a single generation. Other civilizations have been laid low by environmental disaster and social unrest, the Mayans and Mesopotamians and Easter Islanders, but we thought it couldn't happen to us. We had tamed nature.

The woman is prattling on about something. Her voice rises in arpeggios of panic, hands flit wildly about. Sounds like Spanish, but I can't make out a word. I call to Carlos, who has cautiously emerged from his house across the street, machete in hand, to harvest tender lobes from the scrawny prickly pear cactus still holding on in his yard. Even cactus needs water now and again. His eyes rove the street, on the lookout for Scalpers. Just stepping outside these days is an act of courage. He nods at me.

"Hey, man, can you translate for me?"

He gives me a look as he walks over, as if to say, "Why you wanna open this can of worms?" He hears her, too, screaming at lung-top all hours of the day and night. Somehow her cries penetrate the thick walls of our houses. "The lady's begging God for something," he says. "She's pissed off. The lady's off her meds or something. She scares my kids, bro"

"I wonder how she survives out here in no man's land. Why don't the Scalpers or Stalkers get her?"

"Damn, man! Smell her car. Fucking ripe! What's she got to scalp, anyways?"

We had discussed asking the neighborhood patrol to chase her off, but Carlos's wife Miranda chided us, "What kind of assholes are you, wanting to chase off a helpless old woman?" I'm thinking maybe we are assholes to sit and watch her suffer this way. The woman jabbers at us as if we may have some connection to *El Señor* and can deliver him a message.

"She says there's a judgment coming," Carlos says.

"Seems like it has already arrived."

"Yeah, bro, but she sees it sitting on your roof: *El Diablo*. She come over here to keep an eye on it. Looking out for you, bro."

"For me? On the roof of my house? Some kind of demon?"

"Like I said: *El Diablo*. A judgment or warning maybe." Given the smell, he pulls a second mask out of his pocket and puts it on over the first. The intake valve, a huge yellow eyeball against a red background, makes him look like a

Cyclops. His actual eyes leap nervously about above it. When all you can see is a person's eyes, you know what they are feeling. Eyes don't lie. They are more honest than the mouth. "It has glowing purple eyes, she says, and flames coming out of its mouth. The lady's totally brain smoked." Carlos circles a finger around an ear.

"Does this creature mean me harm?" I ask.

She goes into a shouting frenzy when he asks her, repeating "*El Diablo*" over and over, blowing us back a few paces, her dark, sizzling eyes fixed on me. She pats the top of her head and her eyeballs roll up in their sockets as if she's having a fit, displaying an obscene web of blood vessels like she's exposing her naked soul. Carlos shakes his head, not knowing what she's trying to tell us. But I do. Although I can't imagine how she knows since I haven't told a soul. She emerges from her trance and returns to herself.

"She says it's already too late for you and *todo el mundo*, every fucking one of us."

"So we're cursed by the devil or what?"

"It ain't no standard Halloween devil, man. Something to do with climate change and that shit. We're all serving the devil or something. I can't make it out too good. The lady's batshit crazy."

"Maybe. Or maybe she's just seeing what other people refuse to see." I'm thinking all prophets are batshit crazy; it's part of their job. Crazy is creeping up on us all sides. The apocalypse has arrived. It takes fortitude to face it. Most of us prefer to live in denial. "Why my house? No, don't ask her. I don't want to know."

There's nothing unusual about her appearance. Years ago, there were scores of middle-aged Latinx women who looked much like her, round-faced and stout, strolling the streets of L.A. carrying bags of groceries or pushing prams. Now they've been replaced by hungry, rail-thin *bruja*s who will slit your throat for a crust of bread. However, she's frowzy and balding and doesn't wash often, her yellow smock no more than a sack. Who am I to talk? Most of us are in a similar state. If I were a more generous man, I would invite her into my compound for a good scrub. I've only recycled the few gallons of wash water in my tub four times. It's good for a couple more baths. However, I would likely retire the water after she bathed in it. Curiously, her toenails are painted rainbow colors. Where did she find nail polish? Funny what remains in circulation. Her eyes fix on me and won't let go—piercing black lasers that could cut through steel.

"Tell her she's gotta move, Carlos. I don't want her sitting out here bringing the devil or whatever to my roof, sure to attract wolf packs."

He shakes his head. "Nah, man. I don't think she's gonna move. I think we gotta learn to live with it."

"With *El Diablo* sitting on my roof? I don't think so."

He speaks to her again, repeating "*vamos*" over and over and shooing his hands. This elicits another flurry of arm-flailing protests. I throw up my hands and retreat, as does Carlos, muttering to himself, looking nervously about as he crosses the street, like we all do when we're on street side these days, prepared to hightail it to safety. Truly impressive that she lives out here. You hear stories about single walkers living in out of the way places: taking refuge in old Kenneth Hahn Park between recurrent brush fires—even Stalkers won't enter burn zones—or squatting in abandoned buildings. But living on the street in a car? I didn't know there were any of those left. You see the burned-out carcasses of antique RVs which brought refugees from all over the country in the

Thirties and Forties until fossil fuel ran out. No telling what happened to their occupants. A loony tune on the Liberty Network claims they were victims of cannibalism.

OUR CURRENT TROUBLES BEGAN YEARS AGO, centuries really. Some say with the industrial revolution, others the agricultural revolution ten thousand years ago when we started living in fixed abodes and farming. Discontent with what nature provided us, we cut down forests and plowed the earth. We had too many children. Now we live in bunkers and have stopped procreating. Ours is no world to bring kids into. Civilization was advancing full bore, accomplishing wonders, bringing prosperity, exploring space and building artificial brains, then forty years ago it faltered mid-flight. Imagine a bird soaring through the air and suddenly flailing, wings flapping in a panic before it plummets to earth.

Daniel Yashimoto, who lives up on the next block, the last of the Japanese-Americans who once populated the neighborhood, has drawn a graph on his living room wall that shows the upward march of human civilization right into the 2030s when the Chinese became dominant and the vector of upward progress peaked and flat lined, then began its downward plunge like a bull market that suddenly goes bear, dropping from one plateau to another every few years. In 2045 we ran out of fossil fuel. Ten years ago, according to his chart, we had regressed to Pre-industrial Revolution (18th Century), and five years ago to BCE—Before Christian Era (Roman Empire). "Our decline is speeding up," he says.

"So where are we today?"

"Approaching the Paleolithic."

"The stone age? That's a stretch, Daniel."

He frowns. "We're evolving in reverse. We've lost thousands of years of progress in fifty years. The loss of animal species is too depressing to go into." Daniel was a history professor at UCLA until it closed its doors in '51, an expert on fallen civilizations.

"You're an alarmist, Daniel. We have hydrogen-fueled cars now. That's a huge leap forward. We're approaching a zero carbon footprint."

He laughs caustically. "Don't be ridiculous. It's far too late. We lack the industrial base to produce them, infrastructure to support them, and a customer base to purchase them. What good does hydrogen do us now? Fifty years ago maybe, but it's too late for that."

"There are hopeful signs nonetheless. People are fighting back. We haven't lost advanced technology. It's just gone underground. I remain hopeful that it will provide some answers. We've developed the neighborhood patrol network in L.A. to protect us."

He laughs jovially. "Totally outgunned." I think he finds the prospect of apocalypse exciting. What could be more gratifying to a historian than to witness the end of history? "Here we are holed up in our fortresses," he says. "You have to sneak over here at dawn when you know the Stalkers and Night Patrol are least active. If it weren't for the National Guard we would have nothing to eat."

"Should we just give up then? Curl up and die?"

He throws a dismissive hand. Daniel has built what he calls a "Cybersnooper" to monitor the Liberty Network and posts put up by cyberhermits holed up in cabins in the north woods or houseboats out at sea. He has his finger on the information pulse. A valuable guy to know.

Some say trouble begins at birth—it's written into our history. It began with the birth of civilization and will end with its demise. Likely it's written into our genetic code. We may be a canny animal, but we are not wise.

MY BLACKOUTS BEGAN MONTHS BEFORE Mirabella arrived in her red SUV: Mirabella Estragado. She has family in the neighborhood, but they want nothing to do with her since every dream she has about them comes true. They are not happy dreams. It's said she has blackouts before her visions. Maybe that's how she knows I have them, although my blackouts don't come with visions and maybe are better called "blank outs." A segment of my life is snipped out like film left on the cutting room floor, leaving a small gap in the memory flow. I find myself, for example, standing in line at the food distribution center unconscious on my feet, people muttering at me to move up when I return to consciousness after who knows how long.

"What the matter with you, man, standing there like a fucking statue?"

"Sorry," I mumble. "Sorry everyone."

They are carping all the way back to the end of the line two blocks away. "There's hungry people here," a woman shouts. A National Guardsman motions me forward with his assault weapon. He looks like the old Michelin Tire Man in his bulging layers of bullet-proof Kevlar foam. "Okay, I'm going...I'm going. I just needed a moment."

Or I wake up sitting in a living room chair staring into darkness, a book lying open on my lap, a candle flickering beside me. I can't say whether I've been in limbo for just a minute, an hour, or a week. Not even when I look at the calendar, since it's open to a month that I'm fairly certain passed months ago. I check my iGlasses for date and time. They don't tell me much. The batteries are weak; there's no way to recharge them with the power grid down, perhaps permanently. The Scalpers or Night Patrol or the Four Powers have sabotaged it. But there's really no point in knowing it's April 8 at 3:00 P.M. if I don't know when I blanked out. I need to work out a system for keeping track of myself.

So I begin keeping a blackout log, making brief hourly entries:

Monday, April 12, 8 A.M.: *drinking coffee*

Monday, April 12, 9 A.M.: *breakfast dishes done*

Monday, April 12...10 A.M.: *weed the garden*

An empty space signifies that I've had a blank out. But keeping the log makes me feel like I'm living in a prison camp where roll is called every hour. After one blank out, I look back over my log and find Monday, May 15, 9:00 A.M. as the last entry; it's now Tuesday June 26, 6:00 A.M. What the hell? Was I out for six weeks? Wouldn't I die of thirst? Likely I'd had serial blackouts that prevented me from making coherent entries. Some trouble not only has no remedy, but it can't even be comprehended.

So how does Mirabella know about my brain freezes? She surely does, given her head-drooping, eye-rolling mimicry when she sees me. There's a theory that collective ailments manifest in personal ailments. Likely she's attuned to this. She clutched her chest and groaned the day Carlos was translating for me, intuiting his heart condition. But I have no desire to see a doctor even if I could, holed up as they are at UCLA Medical Center behind razor wire fencing and armed guards. Why bother? Just to be told, "We know what you have, but there's nothing we can do about it. Yours is an existential ailment." I could have told them that. Not unlike mankind's collective ailment.

Even before the collapse I had plenty to worry about: my father had dementia, my mother had strokes, my blood pressure was high. I've always had a tendency to obsess about one threat or another since my sister Cassidy disappeared decades ago. Before Denise left me, she complained, "You think of nothing but gloom and doom in your life and everyone else's, Dugan. I can't live with that. I've given up on you. Sorry, but I have. It was a good run, but it's over." The girls, Harmony and Jess, took their mother's side. I haven't seen them in years and don't know what's become of them or their mother. I worry about that. Today, I would bring up Mirabella Estragado and Daniel in my defense: "It's not just me. Gloom and doom are in the air. Only courageous people like those two can face it."

"And it drives them batty," Denise would retort. "Like it has you."

"Daniel's an authority on the collapse of civilizations and Mirabella is a prophetess."

"Right! She sees the devil sitting on your roof."

I ask what she thinks of these spells I'm having—"Are they warnings?"—only partially aware that I'm not actually having a conversation with Denise, only in my head. You invent companions to talk to when you're isolated. No one can live totally alone. So I've got ancient Delgado out in my garden sanctuary, a veteran of World War II and great raconteur. Denise and my sister Cassidy in the front room. Sometimes the girls join us. A young fellow named William in the kitchen, a long-ago occupant haunting the house he was born in. From his clothes and bearing, I would date him back to the 1930s. He knows nothing of our current times or troubles; we never discuss them. He despises nicknames—Bill, Billy or Will—and becomes angry if I use one. "My name is William. Do you want people to call you Dougy?"

"I prefer it to Dugan. My parents named me after the inventor of a biofuel that never panned out, as if to foreshadow that I would be a failure too."

William's laugh is a dismissive snigger. "I haven't the faintest idea what you are talking about." He loves the 'egg foo yum' I cook up in my wok, using sprouts and bok choy from my garden, mixed into commodity powdered eggs and flour from the distribution center.

Occasionally, my sister Cassidy appears in the bedroom. We did bunk beds as kids until I was too old to share a room with my little sister. After she disappeared, I often slept in her bedroom and talked to her as I do now. "What happened to you, Cass? Did you run away? Were you abducted? Did someone hurt you?" She sits mute on the edge of the bed and regards me with an awkward, half-embarrassed smile.

I SNEAK OUT LATE ONE NIGHT to check things out. Will Mirabella's car door be open while she quibbles with *El Diablo* on my roof? I never see him during the day when I venture out. Likely, he's only there at night. I'm eager to catch a glimpse of him. All is quiet but for Mirabella's ratcheting snores through the car's steel skin. It's a cool night, maybe eighty out, likely has cooled off to the low nineties in her car. Up the street, I hear someone singing Paul McCartney's "Let it be." Remarkable, singing the Beatles at three A.M. in no man's land. Seems like an epiphany. I'm grateful for it. Maybe if I could have come out every morning at three A.M. two years ago to let "Let It Be" soak in, Denise wouldn't have left me. Maybe I could have tolerated life, intolerable as it has become.

It occurs to me that The Night Patrol and Scalpers leave Mirabella alone because they fear "crazy" as much as the rest of us do, plus the smell. Or maybe they, too, have a need for sages.

The next night, I'm certain I've had another blank out because I jotted down the time just before placing a home-made bugburger on the grill (pulverized water bugs and beetles compressed in a patty) and came to an hour later at 7:30, still on my feet, hovering over the grill, spatula in hand, preparing to flip the burger, which was reduced to a charred pancake, the kitchen filled with smoke. Had I been frozen like that for an hour? What ailed me? No Alzheimer's symptom I've ever heard of. Not likely a stroke, since I've had dozens of such black outs and would be brain dead by now if they were strokes. Possibly some kind of mental illness? Call it "absence psychosis." When things get dire enough, some of us check out. What's crazy about that?

I go out to Mirabella's rusting antique Isuzu oil guzzler and sit down on my verge, leaning against the rear bumper. The car's metallic skin mutes the interior odor somewhat. The skin has pores and is seemingly organic. She's not fulminating, rather mumbling a meditative chant that sounds more Buddhist than Christian. Vespers perhaps. Paul McCartney isn't on yet, but someone's playing Louis Armstrong's "America...Oh sweet America...." If only we could freeze right here. If only we'd frozen years ago in some fictional version of the America he sings about. If only I could calm my tortured mind and take him for a role model: an African-American singing the praises of a country that enslaved his ancestors.

Maybe it's not about forgiveness so much as about moving on. But moving on to what?

"Mirabella, do you know what ails me?" I ask softly. "What's brought this vexation to sit on my roof and in my head? Something I've done or haven't done? Some selfishness? I could invite you into my home for example; I have two extra bedrooms. It's not right for a man living alone to have two unused bedrooms when others have none. Besides, I could use some human company. I should invite you in and learn proper Spanish. But I'm greedy and foolish. I epitomize mankind's ailments. I'm the canary in our coal mine."

Just then a posse of Stalkers passes down the center of the street, on the other side of the car not twenty feet away, talking loudly so they don't hear me muttering. Thank God. I hunker down, not daring imagine what would happen if they nabbed me. You hear stories. No one ever returns to verify them. I'd sprint for the house, but they'd catch me on legs twenty years younger and said to be more feline than human. They'd ransack my place and carry off whatever they wanted and take me off to trade to the Scalpers, who, rumor has it, use civilians as bait for The Night Crew. Or pass our flesh off as chicken and sell us to the Barterers' Union. Mirabella is at great risk out here on the street under their hungry eyes. Like most places in L.A., my house is a fortress: bars on the windows, electric grids on the doors that give a shock powerful enough to kill a bear. I've reserved my batteries just for them.

Ironically, the mansions in Beverly Hills and Malibu were the first abandoned and ransacked, unprotectable given clerestory windows and half-naked California architecture. Five million dollar homes now occupied by refugees, The Night Crew, and a few brave squatters. The bungalows and Spanish colonials down here in center city are easier to fortify, given thick walls and small windows protected by iron gratings, backyards enclosed by eight-foot high fences topped with razor wire.

I may wait out here until *El Diablo* appears on my roof so I can ask him if he's causing my blank outs. Why me? I'm no guiltier than the next person. Have I offended him? Sure, I don't believe in him anymore than I believe in God. Maybe that pisses him off. But I'm not one of the Koch clan or a kingpin in a bartering cartel. I'm a nobody, a former sociology professor who has written three books that no one has read, who suffers periodic blank outs.

The Stalkers are up at the corner of Jefferson now. I'm afraid they will assault the charging station and expect to hear car tires squeal away into the night, but hear nothing, which is more disconcerting. No telling what silence conceals. I can hear Mirabella talking softly inside the car as if to me. "*Estás vivo es un milagro*," she says. "Life is a miracle." "*Dios es un milagro. El Señor es un gran milagro. El Diablo es un milagro también.*" "God, *El Señor*, the devil are all miracles." "*Todos son milagros.*" "Everything is a miracle." "*Inmigrantes del sur.*" "Refugees from the south." She's speaking Spanglish now, sensing me listening. "*Y los hombres malos* who kill them. I try to speak them. They no listen. *Todo el mundo*, I try to tell. I warning them *el mundo* coming to end. They laugh me. I warning them *El Diablo el destructor* sit on top their head *porque* they make him God. They no listen. *Estoy loca*, they say. I crazy old woman. *Vagabunda, una bruja*. Smell like skunk. *Pero* skunks, '*las mofetas*,' are miracle *también*. They no destroy world. Still, they laugh me. I no *profetisa*. *Loca* bag lady don't know nothing. They make *Dios* in own image y *El Diablo* who sit on *todos* roof in *el mundo*: *Dios de la destrucción.* He hate life and going to destroy. They laugh me. *¿Y tú también?*"

"Not me! I'm not laughing." I know there's not much I can do individually or we can do collectively. It's too late. But we must do something, even if we know it won't help. That's who we are: we break things past fixing, then we try to fix them.

SO I DECIDE TO ABANDON THE CITY. Without a word to anyone. Not Carlos, not Daniel, not my sister in Pasadena (I think she's still there). Surely not Mirabella. Sneak off in the night in my hydrogen-powered Toyota 450H. Take only the necessary: tools, blankets, clothes, as much food as I can cram in. A single canister of hydrogen—all I have. Doubt I'll find any on the road. I estimate a 500 mile range. I will go north to my refuge in the wilds if I can reach it. Leave the house locked up tight. No one will know I'm gone. I debate leaving it standing open for Mirabella and other homeless refugees. But Stalkers would oust them and use it as an operations center. I couldn't do that to the neighborhood. Besides, I might need to return some day.

I'm jazzed when I pull out of my parking cage, like going on a road trip when I was a kid: the open road, adventure, excitement (even knowing the adventures that likely await me out there are none that I want to have). I drive most of the night. If I blank out along the way, I don't notice. I pass refugee camps alongside I-5 in what used to be a clutter of warehouses and light industry on the city's outskirts, a tent compound in a drainage canal. There was bumper to bumper traffic back then; now the interstate is empty and forlorn. I see occasional campfires atop distant buildings, the flames seemingly suspended midair. Such rooftop strongholds are some of the safest places around, protected from Scalpers and The Night Crew by blockaded stairways and booby traps.

You have to be mad to take the I-5 north. No other traffic on the road but for occasional armored cargo trucks. They stop for nothing, crash through barricades and mangle anyone manning them under huge tires, plow aside tractor trailers parked in their path. I slipstream one of them for safety's sake, maneuvering around giant potholes. Campfires burn to my left and right, dark figures carry torches. It's like traveling through another century: no streetlights, no electric lights anywhere. Darkness has reclaimed the world. Road signs have been scavenged for housing or campfires; some hang catawampus from overpasses. In the recent past, you took your life in your hands passing under overpasses in Burbank, used as ramparts to drop heavy stones down on passing cars, some of which remain where they were scuttled. But not enough traffic anymore for the Scalpers to bother dropping stones.

Farther out, thousands of refugees are camped alongside the highway in hovels fashioned of siding torn off abandoned houses in suburbs like Sylmar and Santa Clarita...used to be. Abandoned now. Their owners either fled or died in the pandemics or died of premature old age, given the heat, famine and lack of medical care. Some were likely murdered by Stalkers or desperate refugees who commandeered their homes.

You hear horror stories about refugee gangs that put up roadblocks and pull passengers from their cars and do God only knows what to them. However, they leave the road open at times so foolish travelers like me won't abandon it entirely, else they would have nothing to thieve. I hope lady luck is on my side and I am passing during a fallow period.

I abandon the I-5 near Newhall, since it's said to be impassable over the Grapevine to anything but armored high-wheelers, and take Highway 14 East. What was once a major thruway is dead empty, the pavement torn up in places by asphalt scavengers who extract oil from the tarmac. I creep along the rutted track that remains. The spooky quiet worries me, so I abandon the old freeway near Agua Dulce and take secondary roads through canyons up into the Los Padres National Forest. Back roads are in better condition than freeways, but rarely traveled. Too dangerous. Most people have forsaken car travel altogether, given the scarcity of hydrogen and bio fuels and total absence of gasoline and the danger! How pleasant this route would have been thirty years ago when we still had a fighting chance to stay below three degrees of temperature rise, before the oil cartels went to war against renewable energy companies, before China cornered the hydrogen market and began waging biological warfare on the planet, before back roads became deadly.

I'm hoping to find a hydro station. In the half hour I was able to get on the Undernet before I left, I learned there were a few remaining stations in the region operated by Survival Enterprises. Imagine having the vision in '42 to realize that the shit was hitting the fan for good. Governments and the world economy would soon collapse along with most everything else. Only a privately-held criminal cartel that delivered goods and services governments and traditional corporations could no longer provide would prosper—with its own stores and supply chains, fuel stations and hospitals, currency and security forces, even a legal system. They hired ex-Marines and Navy Seals and enforcers from the old South American drug cartels to police their holdings, armed to the teeth. Survival Enterprises is authoritarian, accountable to no one, run by no one knows who. Essential to those of us who have SurvivalCoin or anything worth bartering. If I am to buy hydrogen, I must buy it from them.

I wend my way back to the 14 beyond Palmdale, one of the fortified towns it's best to avoid, and head toward the Sierras. The demographics change in the mountains. It's mostly white survivalists up here: American-born, well-armed, their shelters more substantial. Dogs bark furiously at me as I pass. It's no man's land up here. You take your life in your hands passing through, and dare not pass through at all if you're dark-skinned. Fear creeps into my bowels. I sit stiffly upright, white-knuckling the wheel. The mountain people have formed clans like the Scottish highlanders; clansmen share the same surname: Trueblood, Avenger, Spartan. The men who stop me at a roadblock wear horned helmets or headdresses fashioned of hawk feathers. They hold Native Americans in high regard since they fought the false American government and the Vikings because they fought most everyone. A man sporting a huge beard, a Confederate flag tattooed across his bare chest, orders me to halt with an upraised palm. He has a flashlight, a rare item likely collected as a toll. I, too, must pay to pass, hopefully not with my hydrogen canister or sleeping bag. "Step out of the car," the man barks. "Hands out wide, palms up."

I nod at stone faces encircling me. "How you fellahs this evening?"

A second man, with a fanged rattler tattooed across his chest, hard eyes me, holding a semi-automatic at port arms. "If I'm going to find a weapon in there, you better tell me now."

"I have a machete for personal protection. You gentlemen having a quiet night?"

"Shut the fuck up! Where you coming from? Where you going?"

"Los Angeles. I don't know where to yet. It's a work in progress."

"You better figure it out real quick. Nobody lasts long out here without a plan."

"Or allies," says a voice from the darkness.

The bearded man's grin is missing teeth. "It's about time you got out of brown town," he says. I decide it's no time to preach racial tolerance. Still, if I had to choose between them, the Confederate is less menacing than the rattler, who watches me closely. "I thought I caught me a foul odor," he says. "Tell you what, Los Angeles, I'll let you keep y'r machete. It's people out here will kill you for the sport of it. But I'll be wanting your jacket."

I take it off, glancing affably about and nodding, hoping they will let me go without taking more. They can charge whatever they like. Nothing you can do about it. I'm wearing my old jacket, having expected to hit toll stops. It's a chilly night; I grip my elbows. Our breath hangs on the air like we're at a border crossing in Manchuria. Everything out here is a touch alien and bygone, a smell of wood smoke and barbecued meat on the air. How long has it been since I've eaten real meat? They gesture me back into the car. The Confederate leans down and speaks *sotto voce*: "They say the Trinity Alps is okay if you can get that far north. Idaho's better. I'd get me to Alaska if I could, but they won't let you in. It's shoot to kill up there, like we ain't got sense to do down here." I nod and thank him for the advice.

No explaining to these people that I didn't flee L.A. for fear of my dark-skinned neighbors, but because of blank outs and *El Diablo* sitting on my roof, because I sensed the whole structure was about to collapse on our heads, and I needed fresh air.

Maybe an hour on, I stop at what was once a rest area to catch a few winks, even knowing I could be accosted by road gypsies or Stalkers and could have my car taken at gun point. But I need sleep. When I emerge from taking a piss behind a Manzanita bush, that ancient relic of a rusted red Isuzu SUV (late 2020's model) that was parked in front of my house in L.A. sits beside my car. Mirabella stands beside it, a shadowy figure in dim moonlight, looking very much like the sorceress she is. "What the hell? How'd you get here, Mirabella? You following me?"

Her eyes fix on mine, full of lunar light. She opens her hands wide to indicate the sky and far horizons, as if to say, *I am everywhere. You can't escape me.* Where did she find gas? How did she avoid the white supremacist toll keepers? Seemingly, the rules don't apply to her. Likely, she's not actually human, not even a seer, but something beyond anything we can imagine. We've reached the point where the unfathomable has become quotidian. Nature, Gods, devils, and our fellow man all working together in a conspiracy of bewilderment.

Mirabella is making another of her unintelligible stump speeches, pantomiming wildly, gesturing at my car, repeating *El Diablo* over and over: *una advertencia apocalyptica.* Informing me, it seems, that the demon Beelzebub, Lord of the Flies, is perched atop my car. I can't see him but do believe I heard his wings flapping in the wind as I drove. There's no escaping him either. Trouble always follows us; it is our destiny. Are Mirabella and her demonic familiar telling me I bear responsibility for what is happening to us? We all do? Humanity owes a debt, and those of us remaining will have to settle up for those who came before, innocent as we may believe ourselves to be of their sins.

I should at least be safe sleeping here with Mirabella parked beside me. An aura hangs around her car. Pentecostal flames dance atop its rusted roof. If you listen hard, you can hear sighs of the dead emerging from inside, like whispering waves washing up on a beach. Every generation, perhaps thirty billion people, all jammed inside that tiny space. A human black hole that has collapsed into such unfathomable density that light and gravity can't escape it, nor history, religion, or hope. Eventually, everything will be sucked inside. Our entire planet. Not even ghouls dare approach that car, certainly not Stalkers or road gypsies or paltry white nationalists with their silly conceits and hatreds. What we're facing now dwarfs all that, all of our previous griefs, hungers, hatreds and fears. All we have strived for is pathetically trivial in the face of the grand apocalypse.

Seemingly, I've been chosen. For what and by whom, I can't imagine. Why me? Perhaps simply because I am your average Joe. It could be any one of us. I am like the jury foreman appointed to represent all jurors—an estimated 2.3 billion of us remaining on earth after the last big pandemic, pneumovirus MINK-16, took out two billion of us.

Will Mirabella continue to accompany me northward? I hope so. I will hone my Spanish so I can understand her and ask why whomever does the choosing chose me. Other cars will queue up behind us. We will form a caravan. Behind them, people on bicycles, in golf carts, on horseback or camelback, on foot, people from earlier times who want to make atonement, our procession extending back into the hazy past. All of us marching toward the unknown, hoping against hope that somehow we can make a difference. Or at least keep homo sapiens and the earth we love alive a little longer.

THE LOS ANGELES CULTURE DEPOSITORY

2038

When he was eighteen, Granny K played Dugan a record on her antique turntable, making him promise he wouldn't tell anyone she owned one. "Scalpers would break in and steal my vinyl to sell to rich collectors. Joplin, The Beatles, The Doors, Dylan...I have it all." The rich were buying up everything, hoarding their bounty for better days they still believed were coming. She led Dugan down to the basement. She was fond of one particular song he often heard her humming: "C'mon people now, smile on your brother...." Something about loving one another right now.

"It's a joke, right?" Dugan said.

"No!" she barked. "We believed it possible. I still do. We were hopeful back then."

"What happened?"

"Greed happened. We have wiped out all the competition and plundered the earth. Our success has been a dismal failure."

The basement shelves were full of canned goods that Granny K had been stockpiling for years: chili con carne, green beans, peaches in syrup, tuna. He would have thought her larder disgusting as a kid, when the stores were stocked with fresh fruits and veggies and the butchers with meat. Then came the emptying. Who would have thought it possible: grocery shelves in America becoming as bare as those in North Korea! Because people were hoarding, rising sea water was swamping ports, making it impossible to offload container ships, diesel fuel for trucks had become prohibitively expensive, and trains were looted by hungry mobs when they pulled into railroad yards; police didn't stop the looting because their friends and families were part of it. And, of course, the endless drought.

Granny K had a knack for mixing together unlikely ingredients in stir fries: canned beets, cherries, sardines, and corn. Quite tasty, actually. Anything from normal times was tasty, even out of cans. Dugan was glad that she'd had the foresight to start hoarding before the shit hit the fan. "How did you know it was coming, Granny K?"

"How could I not know?"

"Most people didn't."

"Most people refuse to see what's right in front of them. Back then their faces were always buried in their cell phones. That's the only positive thing about the present day: cell towers are defunct."

Granny K lived in an old Spanish Colonial in West Adams, some blocks off Jefferson and Crenshaw, which had been blocked off by the homeless. They built a tent city on the Avenue and used the bathrooms in abandoned houses to do their business until Water and Power shut off the water, then did it most anywhere. Granny K often talked about buying an old camper and leaving the city. "It's become unlivable. A couple of grubby Scalpers followed me on my morning walk yesterday. I walked right up to them with my little pen knife and said, 'If you follow me home, I'll make chopped liver of your testicles.' It was worth the fright to see the look on their faces. Eyebrows hopped up in tandem; one mumbled, 'Take it easy, lady. We don't want no trouble.'"

"Damn, Granny! You really did?"

"What else could I do? You have to act crazier than they are. Tell me, Dugan, how's your sex life?" Changing subjects almost mid-sentence like she did.

"Damn, Granny! None of your business."

"I understand you kids have stopped having sex. Good for you. You can't have babies without it, and we don't need more babies in the world."

"I've never had sex," he protested.

"Good for you. Our only hope, you know, is to stop breeding. Eighty percent of us need to die or we don't stand a chance, nor do other creatures. I'll be exiting soon. The earth will be a little lighter for it." Granny K didn't mince words.

"We've used up our share of resources and started usurping others'," she said. "So nature has hit the stop button and shut down humans' sex drive to restore balance. It should have done so years ago. My generation was addicted to sex. We fucked like bunnies. Your generation doesn't want children, so you're becoming infertile. Marvelous! I'm proud of you."

"Except I don't really believe in that. If people don't have kids, humans will disappear."

"Good riddance. In any case, nature is unleashing floods, drought, and earthquakes to restore balance. By the way, I'm off. Did I tell you? I've found a van."

"I thought you were still looking. So you're going to leave your house?"

"I intend to leave it to you. My daughters won't want it. Your parents won't. Laney might take it if it wasn't in the city. Your Uncle Peter! Who knows what's become of him?"

"I'm eighteen. How can you leave it to me?"

"You won't stay eighteen forever. It will be here waiting for you when you're ready." He was about to tell her it wasn't wise to go out on the road at her age: eighty-eight. Nearly impossible to find gas or charge stations or biofuel beyond the suburbs (her van was Triple Fuel). And dangerous out there. Scalpers might steal her van and throw her body in a ditch. But no use giving Granny advice; she'd never taken it in her life. She was something of a role model to him.

2048

IT WAS KNOWN AS THE "Feverish Forties," a little like the 1960's, those old enough to remember them said, but upside down. The Age of Aquarius when anything was possible had been turned on its head. People looked down instead of up. The age of Kali. The age of destruction. We had crossed the 2.5 degree boundary into what many called the End Zone.

Granny K left years ago with a van full of canned goods, headed for a caravan camp up in Humboldt County where it was cooler. She soon dropped off the radar. I moved into her house when I was twenty-one, a year before marrying Denise and having the girls. I was doing my doctorate in sociology, focusing on the mass psychology of desperation, and had become fast friends with Daniel down on the corner of 29th, who had recently gotten an Asst. Professor of history post at UCLA. His specialty was cultural extinction, so we hit it off. One day about a year after Denise left, he said, "I worry about our art and literature. I don't believe we will make it as a species. Maybe crude tribes will survive, but civilization won't. We will want a record of our time here. Not only where we failed but where we succeeded. Any beings that stumble on our planet in the future won't be interested in our science. They will be far beyond us. But they will be fascinated by our art, as we are by the cave paintings at Lascaux. Someone has to preserve our art and literature."

"Isn't that what museums and libraries do: MOMA and LACMA and The Louvre and the Library of Congress?"

He waved a hand at me. "They are being looted. We hear news reports that LACMA and the Central Library are being cleaned out. It's disturbing."

"You can't trust the news. The news is whatever loony propagandists want us to believe."

"We're hearing it from the Truth Keepers and academics. I have it on good authority. Organized raids on LACMA. Cartels make off with the most valuable works and sell them to wealthy collectors, who hope to make a killing selling them back to museums when the climate crisis passes. The fools actually believe it will. The homeless are looting libraries and using books for fuel."

"They burn books?"

"Emily Dickinson and Shakespeare! Our literary *oeuvre* going up in smoke."

"What in hell's wrong with them?"

"They're cold. They burn them in campfires and cooking fires. You know how raw our winters have been. Cold winters, sweltering summers. L.A.'s weather has gone mad."

Wanting to see for myself, I walked over to the tent city on Crenshaw. The stench of raw sewage oozed out of storefronts with their plate glass windows broken out. I had to wear an M-17 respirator mask to tolerate the smell. And for safety's sake. The blogger Sham reported that the air in some homeless camps was contaminated by a pathogen released from the decomposing bodies of prehistoric creatures encased in Alaskan permafrost when it began melting. No one knows how it got to L.A. A zoonotic ailment that consumed the lungs, for which most humans had no immunity. After years of mass death and bodies piling up on sidewalks, homeless folks had built up herd immunity. I had no such immunity.

I'd entered a radically different world just blocks from my own. Like a refugee camp in Chad during the Twenties. They'd long ago stripped the nearby Smart and Final and Fat Town stores and fast food restaurants, and ate well for a time. Had gone mostly hungry since. People lay sluggishly about on filthy mattresses and blankets "salvaged" from nearby houses and apartments, half naked, with open sores on their extremities. Their dead eyes trailed me as I passed through the welter of makeshift shelters and hacking humans. The place reeked of putridity. For some reason, they preferred living out in the open to taking shelter in abandoned houses. I clasped the mask tight to my face; it was all I could do to keep from gagging.

I came upon a hutch fashioned from the entrance and exit signs that once marked the I-10 Freeway. One wall had a huge green "10 East," with an arrow pointing east, the opposite wall "10 West," with an arrow pointing toward the setting sun. Its sloped roof fashioned from a billboard that once towered overhead: "Jesus Saves While Satan Raves!" A hotchpotch of business signs from local storefronts formed the remainder: "Marilyn's Soul Food," "Mel's Texas BBQ." A sign on the hutch door: "No shoes, no shirt, no service." Its owner had a sense of humor.

He sat cross-legged on a pillow in front of the crude structure, a lanky, dark-complected man with a shaved head and a goatee that reached to his navel. "We got ourselves a householder," he called out as I approached. "Share the news with us, young man. Share a pipe." I saw right off that he was camp mayor. Bald children with sunken bellies and huge eyes emerged from their hovels to stare at me. Many of them likely his children.

"Just passing through," I told him.

He laughed. "Ain't nobody like you never just passes through. You come here on business? Maybe to sell me gold watches?" He raised his right arm, decked out from wrist to elbow in gleaming gold Rolexes. "My insurance policy in case they ever worth something again." He motioned me to sit on the filthy sidewalk curb and passed me a peace pipe bedecked with hawk feathers and smelling of sweet hashish. All watched to see if I would remove my mask to inhale or wipe off the pipe stem. Thinking it would be kinder to die from COVID-Upsilon 4 than have my throat slit, I inhaled, while the Mayor grinned. Only canine teeth and incisors remained in the top row. He was a Medieval Lord, attended by women with shaved heads, who made mewling noises as they arranged the robe on his shoulders or filled the pipe.

Huge, fierce-eyed men watched me from the shadows. The Mayor occasionally tossed a bag of chips or candy bar to some ragged denizen from a mound of salvaged goods beside him. They bowed their heads and hurried away. It was a sociologist's heaven: the Middle Ages come back to life. It occurred to me that, if I ingratiated myself to him, I might hang out and get material for a book. He asked where I'd come from. I told him vaguely, not daring give a specific address. Certainly not to him. I'd call him the "King of Crenshaw Avenue" in my book.

"What you do for a living, householder?"

"I teach college and write books."

He thought this hilarious; his bodyguards laughed with him. "I burn books." The Mayor pulled a smoldering copy of *David Copperfield* with a leather cover from a small fire at his feet. I was about to protest when a troop of men and women pushing shopping carts full of clothes, blankets, books, and tins of canned goods came rattling toward us. Food was hard to come by, a valuable commodity since the Port of Los Angeles had been swamped by rising ocean waters and the supply chain began collapsing. Heavily armed sea pirates preyed on the few container ships that dared brave the seas, taking what they wanted and scuttling the ships, crew and all. Semis ferrying food and freight cross-country were hijacked by criminal cartels. Unrelenting drought, the dried up Colorado River, and Northern California's refusal to send water south via the California Aqueduct—keeping it for themselves—nearly ended food production in the Central Valley. Blood was spilled over it. When people in the Owens Valley and elsewhere tried to cut off L.A.'s water supply, heavily armed Los Angeles cops secured the reservoirs.

I thought of Granny K's larder of canned foods in the basement of what was now my house. My emergency stockpile for harder days I knew were coming. I'd be in danger if they got wind of it. I could bring over food for the starving children, but knew the Mayor and his bodyguards would seize and sell it. Here was a secret world hidden in plain sight, which those of us living in what remained of civilization never visited and knew little about.

The Mayor snapped his fingers and pointed toward a huge Army surplus tent, and the mules wheeled their grocery carts into it. "What you do for fun, householder?"

"I save paintings and books like those stacked beside you," I said brazenly. He placed a hand on the books. "Save them for what, householder? What pages we don't wipe our ass with, we use for firewood." His handmaids found this hilarious. Two skinny young men pushed carts full of books into the tent. I made out *Huckleberry Finn* in the pile beside him, and a fat *Calculus for Dummies*. Which gave me an idea.

"Tell you what, I'll trade you your Huck Finn and Jimmy Baldwin's story collection there for some fat old sociology texts I have at home. I could trade you outdated textbooks in exchange for the literature you people collect. They're thicker and burn longer. Plus trash romances and sci-fi. We'd all come out winners. You folks would be helping us preserve culture. You're damn good at scavenging, but you shouldn't be burning our cultural legacy to make a pot of beans."

He squinted at me as if he couldn't believe that I was lecturing him, then smiled ear to ear, looking like a feral cat given gleaming canines in the top row. "You gotchou a attitude, householder." Nodding at his bodyguards, who nodded accord. "I like a man with attitude. Ain't never met a householder with attitude before. That got me impressed. You come here where you ain't wanted and tell me I can't be burning our *cultural legacy*, whatever the fuck that is. You gotchou a pair, Professor. You ever seen that?" he asked a giant bare-chested white man, huge arms crossed over a sumo wrestler's belly, swastikas tattooed on his biceps, a human skull on his forehead, chief honcho of the bodyguards, the *Jefe*. He stood glaring at me.

"I don't mean any disrespect. I just see an opportunity for us both." I was way out on a limb, promising him something I wasn't sure I could deliver.

"I can't decide if you crazy stupid or crazy smart some way I don't know nothing about. Bring me them books, Professor, then we can talk."

"The name's Dugan."

He shrugged. "I know you got one."

I hurried away, feeling like a reprieved man, knowing he would send people to follow me home. A group of young boys worked as a tag team, one took the lead for a time, then passed it on to another, while the others dropped out of sight, like a pack of coyotes chasing down a rabbit. I went in the opposite direction from home, toward Adams, speed-walking east without plan or destination. Just knew it would be disastrous if they learned where I lived. They would break in and take the stacks of books Daniel and I had salvaged thus far, likely find the cache of canned goods in the basement. People were killed for less. As I was crossing the Hoover Pedestrian Mall on the USC campus, a campus cop halted the lead boy and sent him packing, allowing me to get away. They were picky about who they let on campus.

WE GOT BUSY AFTER THAT. No time to lose. No one realized it would happen so fast. Once things started sliding downhill it became an avalanche. Some extinctions had occurred in the blink of an eye: an asteroid hitting the earth, a mega volcano. The Sixth Extinction wasn't much slower. Not the extinction of Homo Sapiens, not yet, but of our culture and way of life and much of the natural world we love.

We focused first on LACMA—the Los Angeles County Museum of Art. Daniel heard from a colleague that it was being stripped of masterpieces by the Free-Market Cartel that fenced art for wealthy clients. Approaching the post-modern museum that looked like a graceless wing fallen to earth late one afternoon, we found doors standing wide open. The nearly-bankrupt city was forced to lay off museum guards and curators, along with librarians. Volunteers filled in for a time, but were run off by cartel heavies and scavengers, one of whom slunk out of an entrance carrying a painting wrapped in brown paper, throwing us a wary glance. Were the homeless burning paintings or hanging them in their hovels? I sensed we were being watched.

Inside, paintings and prints deemed of little value littered museum floors, with their protective wrappings torn off. Empty frames leaned against walls, canvases cut crudely out of them and rolled up for easy transport. Heads and hands were hacked off statues too heavy to haul away. Storage vaults were looted. The museum's masterpieces mostly gone: Picasso's "Weeping Woman with Handkerchief," Thomas Eakin's "Wrestlers." Half-naked men grappling on a mat likely appealed to the thieves. A ghostly rectangle, a shade lighter than the wall surrounding it, remained in place of Cezanne's "Still Life with Cherries and Peaches," one of my favorites. But, remarkably, Diego Rivera's "Flower Day" still hung on a wall. Thieves likely thought it painted by a child, given its deceptive simplicity. Nearby, hung Magritte's "*Ceci n'est pas une pipe*" ("This is not a Pipe"), which they considered too mundane to be valuable. Winslow Homer's "Cotton Pickers" was leaning against a wall. Cartel thieves probably doubted wealthy white collectors would want a painting of two African-American women in a cotton field. Daniel clapped his hands for joy and cried, "Thank God for ignorance." We grabbed the Rivera, Magritte, and Homer and went for the exit. Daniel stumbled over a small painting on the floor. It had been trod on, canvas torn away from the frame: Goya's "And So Was His Grandfather." Looters apparently had no use for the man with a donkey's head. Daniel fell to his knees and clutched it to his chest. "We have saved a Goya," he whispered.

We exited to dusk and wound through the park, skirting tents of the homeless and ducking behind trees, looking back to make sure we weren't being followed, then sprinted across a nearly deserted Wilshire Boulevard for Daniel's van, parked on a side street, with our loot. Ours was surely one of the largest art heists in history and the only one ever done in a good cause.

We stashed salvaged paintings in my basement and the fortified garage behind Daniel's house. Made repeated forays to the museum. Soon realized our storage vaults were too dank, given the atmospheric rivers that passed through sporadically and sent trickles of water down basement walls. Ours was the strangest of climes: severe drought interspersed with wanton downpours. My living room was filling up with books recovered from branch libraries and bookstores, stacked floor to ceiling. Daniel said, "I used to think it tragic that people had stopped reading. Now I'm delighted they did, else they would have stripped libraries and bookshops bare and left nothing for us. There's an irony for you: books saved because no one wants to read them."

Finding them was no easy task. The big Central Library on 5th Street near skid row had been stripped bare but for a twenty volume *Oxford Unabridged Dictionary* and a set of *Encyclopedia Britannica*, circa 1986. Maybe the barbarians thought a record of human history should remain. But the branch library on Jefferson near Arlington was untouched and the Baldwin Hills Branch nearly so. We pulled van load after load out of them—the complete works of Shakespeare and Twain, plus science and business texts, hundreds of cheap sci-fi and romance novels to trade with the Mayor of Crenshaw Avenue for the classics his people collected. Daniel insisted we save a sampling of them. "We can't preserve culture, especially American culture, without business texts and sappy romances. Culture comprises both the masterpiece and the mundane."

But where to store it all? I had to leave corridors between stacks of books to reach my front door and bedroom as it was. Daniel discovered a secret cavernous vault beneath Royce Hall on the UCLA campus, converted to an air raid shelter in 1942, buttressed by concrete arches to withstand a direct hit, and connecting to the legendary tunnel system running under parts of the City of Angels like the Roman catacombs. Few campus authorities knew it was there (Daniel never told me how he did), directly below one of the most famous concert halls in the country, although there had been no performances there in years given the pandemics that regularly assaulted us. No one could afford to attend them, anyway. The vault provided thousands of square feet of storage, more if we extended into tunnels, and would withstand the ravages of time better than our home storerooms.

We were determined to bring out as many works remaining at LACMA as possible. We had to remove some large paintings from their frames and roll them up; some sculptures were too heavy. We became known to regulars who warned us not to be greedy. The Cartel was sure to notice. We ducked into restroom stalls when Cartel scalpers appeared, even though we dressed grubbily enough to pass as hungry derelicts. Curators from the Getty were likely among the looters. That fortress on the hill, housing van Gogh's "Irises" and Leonardo da Vinci's "The Last Supper," was well-guarded.

We varied our delivery times to the vault so campus guards didn't become suspicious. Students posed a problem, given the frequency of our deliveries, even though we offloaded at a loading dock behind the building once used to bring in props and pianos. Campus officials would likely nix our project if they got wind of it. To reach the grotto, we had to maneuver down a steep, narrow flight of stairs, assisted by some of Daniel's most-trusted grad students, who were as passionate about cultural preservation as we were.

At first, the Mayor of Crenshaw Avenue kept his end of the bargain, trading classics for our lesser works, although he'd developed a taste for J.G. Ballard novels. "That motherfucker's crazy." We began to notice other camp dwellers reading, beginning to find value in books beyond warming their feet, perhaps wanting to know how others faced hardship. "I don't know if our efforts will succeed," Daniel said as we arrived at 29th and Crenshaw one afternoon to find a camp guard engrossed in *Lord of the Flies*. Daniel had to honk twice to get his attention. "The paintings and books may deteriorate, but at least we've made some new readers."

We didn't notice the boy on motorized roller skates following us after our delivery. Generally, Daniel took a roundabout route and drove crazy fast, while I sat in back keeping a lookout for followers. But we were in a hurry to pick up some paintings we'd left at my house and get them to the vault before dark. He drove straight to my place. I saw the roller skate paparazzi whiz past, his keen eyes surveying my house, no doubt shooting pictures with his iGlasses. Just foolish paranoia, I told myself. Nothing to worry about.

Returning from delivering paintings to the vault, we found my front door open, the Mayor's people carrying books and cans of food out to shopping carts. They had used a cutting torch to take off the fortified steel door. Neighbors I'd known for years stood on their front lawns watching, afraid to intervene. "Assholes," I shouted at them. I called 9-1-1 but got a taped message: "All operators are busy at this time. If you are calling about a crime-in-progress the police will respond by order of severity." Meaning never. I ran into my house, knocking books out of mules' hands, shouting, "I thought we had a deal." The Sumo wrestler *Jefe* emerged from the kitchen and slammed his forehead against mine. I staggered back, my visual field gone blood red for a moment. Close up, he looked like a walrus; stiff whiskers bristled under his snout. "We don't do deals, householder." Dragging me by the back of the neck into the kitchen. Cupboards stood open; the floor was littered with broken glass. They had emptied storage bins of potatoes, dried corn, and peanuts, and cupboards of cans. He pulled me over to a door on one side of the kitchen that opened onto a brick wall. It had once opened onto a staircase leading down to the basement, but Granny K blocked it off and dug a secret entry to her food cellar in the backyard, fearing something like this could happen. I'd covered the hatch with a rug littered with dirt and dried grass.

"What the fuck's this, householder? What's behind the wall?"

"I've always wondered that myself. A door opening onto a brick wall...weird. It was like that when I got the house." I sounded convincing since it wasn't altogether a lie.

"Maybe it leads to a basement?"

"Not as far as I know." He studied my face in the dim light of the ceiling fixture's single bulb (I had to conserve what with electricity at forty dollars per kilowatt hour), nodding his head and frowning. Pulling me to the back door, he nearly threw me down the steps into the yard.

"What's all this shit?"

"My garden."

"I see it's a fuckin' garden, householder. What you need it for?"

"To grow food. That's where the potatoes and corn and peanuts you stole come from."

He regarded me quizzically. "Why grow it when you can buy it? Ain't you a big shot professor?"

"I can't afford much on my salary. I'm not a rich man."

"You got more potatoes and carrots back there?" He snapped his fingers and sent a couple of boys into the garden to see, then dragged me down tidy rows by the nape of the neck, stomping beet, chard and lettuce greens underfoot. "What's this crap?"

"You're trampling my food. If you're going to starve me to death, you might as well shoot me." I could see the boys had no idea what they were looking for, which gave me an idea. "Listen," I said, "you need to get the Mayor over here. I can arrange for you folks to get many times more than what I grow here."

He guffawed. "How the fuck you gonna do that, householder? You grow any smoke?"

"You could. I can teach you how. That's what I want to talk to the Mayor about."

He stood studying me a time, interested now. The last pink hint of sunset glazed his bald head. The night would be dark. They would cut off the power at nine, and stars would appear like magic across the canopy of sky overhanging the city as if we'd gone back hundreds of years. He snapped his fingers and motioned his people out of the garden. "You may be smart, Professor, but if y'r fucking with us y'r gonna wish you was stupid."

Thank God Daniel hadn't played hero and come looking for me, giving the *Jefe* cause to shoot us both. They pulled him from the van and made off with it—fortunately empty—and left Daniel sprawled on the dirt yard, terrified. I helped him up. "No worries. I have a plan."

NEXT DAY, I TOOK MY PROPOSAL to the Mayor, who grinned hugely as I approached, displaying his incisors. "Well, looky who the cat dragged in. You lose something, householder?" His baldy bodyguards laughed with him. It even brought the hint of a smile to the *Jefe*'s face.

"I came to offer you a better deal than the first—for all of us."

He tapped incisors against his bottom teeth. "Go on, I'm listening."

I told him that in exchange for my books and Daniel's van back, I would teach his people how to grow food. "You folks don't have to go hungry. You can grow all the food you want: potatoes, corn, beans, carrots, peanuts....even smoke. Grow it and sell it if you want to. There's plenty of demand. I'll teach you how. Plenty of fertile land: center strips and city parks and abandoned properties. Some of us in the neighborhood are already doing it. We call ourselves the West Adams Grange. You can grow year-round in L.A."

The Mayor was skeptical, but he was listening. Hearing me talking about food, his hungry people gathered around. "You folks could help us tear down abandoned structures and use the space to garden. We lack the manpower to do it alone. There's power in numbers. Authorities won't dare try to stop us. Orange County Proud Boys won't dare raid us. We'll help you out with starter seeds and cuttings and give you some of our bounty to tide you over until your first crop comes in." I knew transforming scavengers into urban farmers was a stretch, but when the Mayor raised an index finger, like an antenna to gauge the sentiment of the crowd, his people mumbled assent. "You better come through, householder. We know where you live."

The West Adams Grange provided seeds and taught them how to plant and fertilize and compost. We tore down a tract of decrepit garden cottages on Edgehill, belonging to the city, and cut the walls down to their foundations to form giant raised beds, dug cisterns to store rainwater from atmospheric rivers that occasionally passed through, lining them with Spanish tiles salvaged from roofs. The Crenshaw Avenue crew pilfered chickens and goats from somewhere, which we penned in the backyards of abandoned dwellings, along with turkeys and hogs. One of Daniel's friends at UCLA estimated that a quarter million cubic tons of organic vegetables were grown by urban farmers in L.A. in 2049.

The Crenshaw Avenue camp shrank as inhabitants took up residence in deserted houses and apartments. Agriculture was domesticating them as it had homo sapiens ten-thousand years ago. Leroi Phipps and his sons built a colonnade, like those once common in Spain and Arabia, to provide natural air conditioning when breezes flowed through and were cooled by the shade. People hung out under it on scorching hot days. We were reinventing civilization.

It seemed too good to be true, like a Fifties Hollywood movie. Formerly homeless folks built makeshift showers and outhouses and took pride in their new homes. No one from the neighborhood pilfered from our gardens since produce was shared communally. We had goat and chicken BBQs and drank homemade beer. People stopped leaving the neighborhood and outsiders wanted in. Call it end-zone gentrification.

The greatest danger was Proud Boys and the Liberty Patrol, who came in from the outer rings on "meat and potato" runs. Our night watch could fend off city marauders, but were outgunned by the rednecks and fled when raiders came for our bounty. Leroi Phipps and his sons designed an air raid siren and walkie talkies so the night watch could inform Leroi about a raid. He would sound the alarm, and men and women would pour into the street, armed with axes, knives and our few firearms.

THINGS CHANGED QUICKLY IN that critical time. Daniel and I sensed that the cartel was onto us. We went rarely and furtively to LACMA early in the morning, parking the van close so we could make a run for it. Finding heavily-armed guards in camo gear posted at the doors one morning, we retreated. As we rounded a corner toward Daniel's van, we watched it go up in flames.

Two nights later, I was on night watch with Julio, a formerly homeless man, wiry and high-strung, chain-smoking marijuana, our two big Alsatians, and a few of the boys when a pickup came racing toward us down Edgehill. I tried to alert Leroi, but the walkie talkie was dead. Men in the pickup bed wore life-like masks bearing the visages of their favorite fascists: Hitler, Joe Stalin, and Trump. The dogs leapt for them. On a superhero high, Julio tried to pull a man out of the pickup. The raiders clubbed him and the dogs with rifle butts, then kicked the dogs lying on the ground to a pulp. Julio nearly so. There was nothing the boys and I could do but watch as they held us at gunpoint and stripped the biggest community garden of marijuana, root crops and corn, then set the corn stalks on fire. By then, food of any sort was going for hundreds of dollars a bushel. Remarkably, they let us live. Remarkably, too, the L.A. Fire Department sent an engine to douse the blaze that had spread to nearby houses. Of all public agencies, they were the most tenacious.

I thought I recognized the voice of the huge gang leader, wearing a gorilla face mask. It was the *Jefe*. Possibly, the Mayor resented his former followers' growing hunger for independence and a roof over their heads, but it made little sense for him to rob us. We had made him one of the richest turf lords in Los Angeles. He taxed everyone in the neighborhood, collecting food and marijuana and setting up one of the city's few remaining grocery stores and pot shops. He wouldn't kill the goose that laid the golden egg. Likely the *Jefe* had gone rogue.

Then one night Daniel and I visited our basement grotto below Royce Hall. Above its entrance was a wooden sign carved by one of his grad students: "*the Los Angeles culture depository.*" The door was padlocked. So we were amazed to find the Depository ransacked, many masterpieces gone, along with leather-bound antiquarian books, and dozens of lesser paintings. They had come in through the tunnels, perhaps tipped off by a campus guard or student. We sat on the floor. Demoralized. Speechless.

I kept watch in the Depository on nights following, along with a couple of grad students, to guard what remained, armed with the old deer rifle my father had inherited from his. We packed the used hydro-van I'd bought with the last of my savings with rubble from the cottages we had torn down—chunks of concrete, bricks, and cinderblocks—and trucked them to campus to plug the tunnel. Perhaps two tons by the time we'd finished.

I will never forget Daniel's expression that day when we had secured the Depository. He sat on a stack of encyclopedias, all the energy drained out of him, and looked up at me with the most doleful face I've ever seen, uncharacteristic of buoyant Daniel. "You realize there's no saving anything anymore. We are going to lose it all."

"We've done our best," I said, not wanting to believe him. We had, after all, managed to feed the neighborhood. Had changed people's lives. We had a good start on the Depository. We had butterflies and bees visiting our garden plots. Many nights, we sat out on our front lawns, drinking homemade beer and singing old Woody Guthrie songs, looking up at a miraculous, star-filled sky above the dark city, feeling something like hope.

DR. DOOM AND THE MESSENGER

Dr. Doom entered the classroom after students arrived and sat in back, planting shoe heels on the desk in front of him. A few students, including Minah, snipped glimpses of the odd man at the rear of the room, eyes dodging forward again when he returned their gaze. A bald swath ran down the center of his head like a landing strip, a severe little beard pointed down from his chin like a crooked finger. His eyes sweltered. Minah felt them branding the back of her neck. Too old to be a fellow student and clearly not the professor, who would be at the front of the classroom looking over the roll sheet or sitting on the edge of the desk greeting them with a cordial smile. The girl next to Laney leaned over to whisper, "Who's that creep?"

"The inspector," she whispered back, sensing his eyes on her.

"The End of History" course was offered by the Sociology Department to be taught by a visiting professor who held doctorates in history and evolutionary biology and had written thirteen books with depressing titles such as *How Civilizations Die* and *Nothing To Eat*. An intellectual jack of all trades. Minah was excited about the class and fixated on the subject it addressed: global warming and mass extinction, perhaps both of animals and humans.

A fidgety student entered fifteen minutes late, muttering about his car not starting. The man in back barked, "You are late, young man! Next time you're out of my class." Then snapped, "Sit down!" at two students who rose to leave, fed up with whatever game the professor was playing. They sat instantly; his was not a voice to defy. He began speaking from the rear of the room, slowly making his way to the front. "You see our problem? Three examples of it already and we've just begun. Impatience is the byword of the day, an inability to tolerate frustration or even notice what's right before your eyes—classic hallmarks of a doomed civilization. We are an impatient species, a greedy species, a species that can't ever get enough. Frugality is an axiom in the animal world that humans don't accept. We are addicted to growth. More is better. Bigger is better. What a silly idea 'trading up' is in the natural world. Does a bear keep trading up to a bigger den? But you three—" pointing at the triplet of violators "—will devote your lives to it! Do you realize, kids, that four-hundred parts of carbon per million has long been considered the red line. We crossed it years ago and are speeding toward two degrees of warming, likely four by century's end. That will be catastrophic, the end of human history."

Minah was both scandalized and intrigued. Professors don't attack students in the first few minutes of class or talk down to them with disdainful relish as he clobbers them with bad news. He stood on one foot at the front of the room, the other planted against the wall behind him. His six-foot frame swayed to the fury of words pouring from his mouth; he teetered as if in danger of toppling over. He assaulted them with a nonstop rush of bad news: species die-off, humans and their livestock accounting for 95% of the biomass of mammals, loss of natural habitat, clear-cutting old growth forests at the rate of twenty-thousand acres a day and destroying the lungs of the planet, pollinator die-off, microplastics in the bloodstream of all living things, wildfires doubling in ferocity every year in the West, hurricanes on the gulf coast, floods in Bangladesh, pollution in Beijing, hundreds of millions of climate refugees pouring over borders into wealthier countries. "Soon people will be shooting them down at the border, including some of you... because you will, kids. Ten, twenty years from now, you will. On behalf of my generation and those that came before, I apologize for putting you in this horrible position. It delights me to hear you're no longer having sex. That's hopeful. In my day, we couldn't get enough. Damn fools. There are now eleven billion of us on the planet. It can't accommodate so many; there isn't enough food and water. Go infertile, kids, stop dropping brats."

Around Minah students were stunned, like boxers on the ropes. The girl who'd whispered "creep" was on the brink of tears. Most slumped in their chairs under the heavy hand of dread. Minah felt calm, even relieved. She liked it when people told the truth, no matter how distressing. If you don't know what you are facing, you can't hope to face it. Her parents had refused to accept it when her younger sister went missing, so made little attempt to find her. She couldn't forgive them for that. She hated avoidance.

Most students left class downcast. A half dozen stayed behind to tell Dr. Doom they were dropping. "I don't sign drop slips," he barked. "I'll have to flunk you. Do you think the climate permits us to drop out? You are the kind of people who need to start listening."

If his intention was to stir debate, he succeeded famously. She hung out with three of her classmates at the student union after class discussing his lecture, one a survivor of the East Bay Complex Fire that had destroyed the Oakland and Berkeley Hills and run clear to Walnut Creek, killing eighty-thousand people. "I'm going to hate this class." He sighed.

"Me too." Minah agreed, "that's why I'm staying in it."

"That makes no sense," a girl snorted from a nearby table.

"It does if you're scared all the time but don't know what you're scared about."

"I learned a lot from the fire, but don't know what to do with it," the boy said. "I hope to get some ideas from Dr. Doom's class."

"'Dr. Doom!' I love it," a boy nearby cried. "'Dr. Doom and Gloom.'"

"I hope he has solutions," Minah said. "The only thing better than someone who knows what's broken is someone who knows how to fix it."

"It pissed me off that he kept calling us 'kids,'" the girl said.

"Many of you," Dr. Doom warned them in the second class, "will join bizarre cults as rising seas flood coastal cities and blazing heat distorts and dulls your brains and makes zombies of you. When your brains are melting in their skull pans, you will think nothing of running down pedestrians in crosswalks. Fortunately, there will be no cars and few pedestrians."

"Not me!" Minah called out. "I hate cults. A cult stole my sister from me."

AUNT LANEY HAD NOT SEEN the boy who called himself "Moss" for some time, but felt certain that he was still combing the mountain for supplies to pilfer after fire destroyed every cabin on the mountain except hers. He had promised to leave her in peace since she was planting trees to help refurbish the decimated forest. Perhaps that was why the burning forest had spared her house, since trees, she believed, possess hive intelligence. She must case her neighbors' survival bunkers for supplies before Moss and others from below beat her to it. Nothing remained to eat on the mountain but what dead neighbors had stored in their caches. She had at most three months of food and water remaining in hers. Moreover, survivors might still be trapped in underground sanctuaries and would need help getting out.

She started with the O'Ryan place nearby. Nothing was left of the house but a few charred studs rising from the ashes and blackened rafters arranged in a grid atop a mound of cinders as if the roof had come down in a unit. Spanish tiles lay in a jumble one side. What appeared to be an AC unit had melted into a solid puddle. Fierce Santa Ana winds blowing over the bare mountains these past weeks had blanketed everything in sand and dust. However, winds blew from the west now rather than the east, depositing the Valley's topsoil on slopes overlooking it. Everything gone cockamamie and unnatural. It amazed her how quickly civilization, which had taken fifty-thousand years to build, could collapse. They were watching it happen in real time. A few hundred years from now—hopefully after forests had come back—you might walk over this spot and not know that any human habitations had been here. She found this a strangely comforting thought.

She dug and poked in the area where she surmised the O'Ryan's bunker would be, but found no trace. So she went down the mountain to Tom and Liberty Cotton's place. They surely had a well-stocked bunker; they were survivors. Tom's backhoe was gone. Likely he'd lowered its blade and plowed a path through the burning woods, fleeing the mountain, with his crippled wife riding in the raised backhoe bucket behind him. Laney had spent many summer evenings with Liberty drinking home-made juniper gin while Tom cleared the road leading down to the Valley, the single remaining escape route. Remarkably, the two patio chairs they sat on remained in pristine condition on their scorched deck overlooking the Valley. An omen. Over the years, fewer and fewer lights were visible below in what had once been a grid of electrified jewels extending into the distance before the power started going out. Fewer and fewer cars crawled along roadways. One by one, lights blinked out until nothing remained but pulsing campfire clusters blurred by smoky haze in survivalist compounds. Civilization was shutting down.

The San Jacinto Valley had long been home to hapless itinerants, ne'er-do-wells, Jesus freaks, aging health nuts, Neo-Nazi loonies and left-wing paranoiacs. If you wanted a catalog of the cultural fads of the past fifty years, you couldn't do better than the Valley, which Liberty called "California's wet dream." A curious name for one of the driest places in the state.

Other than the chairs, nothing remained but ash two feet deep. The hatch opening onto the Cotton's underground bunker stood wide open. Cleaned out, she knew, before looking into it. Hopefully by Tom and Liberty before they fled. More likely by Moss and his pals or other scavengers from the Valley. "I'll have to abandon the mountain soon," she told that empty hole. "But go where?" In time she would surely locate the O'Ryan's stash. Even so, there was little hope of holding out for more than a year or two. When the future becomes an inverted question mark, it's hard to sustain hope. But hard to go on without it.

Reaching the first burned-out cabin on Ponderosa Lane, she heard something scurry away over cinders with a rustling metallic sound and saw movement in a stand of charred trees below. Whether animal or human she couldn't tell. Seemingly, she spooked it and it fled.

You would expect Armageddon to manifest in monotonal black and white, but the fire's hot breath had littered the ground with scorched pine needles that formed rust-red rings at the base of blackened snags. Cinders were scraped away from an area below the cabin, likely by whatever scurried away. No doubt searching for food and water, but looking in the wrong place, she saw at once, noting the bunker's air intake pipe affixed to a stump above an abbreviated incline. The bunker wasn't underground but mined into the hillside, its hatch cleverly concealed by a latticework of charred branches cemented together with baked red clay. Unable to open the hatch by hand, she found a galvanized pipe in the cabin rubble and pried it open. The putrid stench of a dead animal sent her reeling backward, a hand over her mouth. Whoever was left trapped inside had likely died of smoke inhalation weeks ago.

She left the hatch open to air the bunker out and hurried uphill for her pistol. No doubt it was feral dogs—some of the only wildlife remaining on the mountain—that had scratched at the dirt in search of food. A devious hybrid of doomed civilization, they could be deadly dangerous, as were human scavengers. If she was to compete with them for the stash, she must be armed. The rotting corpse guarding the bunker wouldn't keep them away for long.

THE LAB WHERE MINAH WORKED tracking fungal infections had closed a month ago. Such infections, which had wiped out most cold-blooded amphibians, including frogs, were now sickening humans. Potentially more deadly than SARS-MinkX that had killed an estimated one-fifth of the earth's population. Warm-bloodedness had long protected people from fungal infections. But now that it was getting warmer, fungi had mutated to withstand higher temperatures in hosts' bodies, beginning in the damp Indian subcontinent and quickly spreading around the globe—*Candida auris Cryptococcus* in particular, which was much like Ebola. Victims died within thirty days. There was no known treatment. In Southeast Asia, they used caustic fungicides to save babies who were particularly prone to fungal infections, but these were often as deadly as the fungi.

Years ago, Dr. Doom had warned about exotic infections. His gloom saying had inspired in her a realization that she wanted to be part of the solution rather than a helpless bystander. So she became a biologist. But labs, like hospitals, were closing from lack of funding and, increasingly, of staff, who regularly fell victim to the lethal ailments they were trying to cure.

She had been on the road since the lab closed, looking for... she didn't know what exactly. Renewed purpose? Safe haven? She thought of seeking shelter at her brother Dugan's place in L.A., but the dying city was best avoided. Moreover, she hadn't heard from Dugan in years. He could have moved or might even be dead. So she set out for her Aunt Laney's cabin in the San Jacinto Mountains. She had visited her aunt as a girl and loved the serenity and sense of self-reliance in the mountains. People up there were as resilient as the ponderosa and Jeffrey pine trees that battled drought and bark beetle infestation, which was itself like a fungal infection. Beetles devoured living tissue under the bark, leaving behind hillsides of dead orange trees.

She followed highways south on foot, sticking to drainage ditches paralleling roadways, ready to dive into a culvert if a vehicle approached, or finding her way through chaparral or forest along the road. It was tough going, but it shielded her from armored Patriot Patrol personnel carriers that trolled the roads in search of climate refugees, Scalpers, and anyone else they could lay their hands on. No telling what they would do to her: swap her to Scalpers for one of their own, sell her to a cartel, rape her, or, if she was lucky, just take her rucksack. Her sister Cassidy was kidnapped by a white slaver cartel years ago. But patrols passed rarely and no one else dared travel the highways. The Patriot Patrol owned the roads.

Early one morning somewhere near Riverside, she heard an angry swarm of Africanized bees, a furious droning that shivered the air. From behind a bush, she watched the swarm circle high in the air: a pulsing, living organism, swerving side to side, fraying in tatters, then coming together again in a tight spinning ball, forming one single entity with a multiplex intelligence comprised of many individual neurons. Fascinated and terrified, she watched that living nebula perform a circle eight, then hover high above ground directly overhead as if sensing her presence. The swarm plunged toward her. Fleeing, she knew, would further infuriate the swarming beast, but instinct told her to run. Incredibly, a stagnant pool stood at the mouth of a culvert just ahead. She dove in headfirst and frantically smeared her body with glaucous muck that stank of putrescine and cadaverine, those toxic amines she knew well from the decaying flesh of test frogs at the lab. The pond was surely infected with the deadly fungi that abounded in all stagnant water now. But better to die in thirty days than the agonized minutes she would have if the swarm got her. Smelling swamp scum that reeked of death, it veered away.

Rising from the sludge, Minah passed through a haze of mosquitoes vibrating above the inky surface of the pool, slicked with prismatic light that opalesced in a liquid rainbow over the opaque water. A seductive but devious beauty, since mosquitoes posed the deadliest threat in the animal kingdom—carriers of West Nile Virus, Dengue Fever, and malaria. But nearly comatose in the heat, with barely strength enough to hover, they left her alone. She wiped the sludge off her skin with a t-shirt and much of the little water she had left.

Sometimes in the early morning long before dawn she walked barefoot on the tarmac. At this coolest time of day, the temperature often dropped into the eighties. It was dangerous, but she surmised that she would feel the vibration of an approaching vehicle in the soles of her feet and could get off the road before headlights appeared.

She passed through mostly-abandoned suburbs on the outskirts of Hemet on high alert. During normal times, housing tracts had metastasized across the Valley. Now they were disappearing under sand dunes birthed by fierce Santa Ana winds. Ozymandias California style. Chaparral sprouted on rooftops and mesquite invaded living rooms occupied by snakes, lizards, rats and the skinny coyotes that fed on them. She was careful to avoid hills of fire ants that could set her feet ablaze. The hot new world was birthing the age of arthropods. An eerie chorus of yipping coyotes echoed through derelict McMansions. "Hurry," she urged herself, "if you don't want them to make a meal of you." She held a golf putter she had found in the rubble at the ready.

Without warning, a hydro-van leapt around a corner and silhouetted her in its headlights. Bare-chested men and women in loincloths leapt out and surrounded her, crouched and armed with thick clubs as if she were a dangerous animal, surely one of the neo-indigenous cults she'd heard tales about, but had dismissed as one of the end-time urban legends that abounded, including about Scalpers who were said to dine on human flesh. A tall man with a deeply lined face got out and approached her. A braided blond beard hung down his bare chest, his hair also done up in fastidious braids. Muscles of his powerful body were delineated as if in an anatomical chart, each distinct and seemingly oiled. His eyes were spectral moons aglow in the headlights. "What do we have here, barefoot and ready?" he asked. His followers stood up straight, regarding her with slack expressions. "You know, sweetheart, there's packs of wild dogs roaming these precincts and the Burning Crew that torched houses over yonder." She made out their glistening skeletons in the moonlight. "It's a dangerous place to be."

"I only wanted," she spluttered, "I'm just trying to reach—"

"Let's say we give you safe harbor, what can you offer us?" It didn't seem he was giving her much choice: join them or God-only-knows-what.

"—trying to reach my aunt on the mountain," she continued.

"On the mountain? Y'r aunty is up on the mountain?" His eyes widened. "Tell you what, she's burnt toast. Nobody could have survived the last fire."

"Last fire?" she asked.

"Three months back. There's still ash blowing. They say there's bunkers where people stored their food up there. One of these days we will go up and see for ourselves. Dead people don't eat." His followers found this funny, whether he intended them to or not.

"You think my aunt's dead?"

He shrugged. "Not saying one way or the other. I presume." Light from the headlamps refracted off his eyes, throwing spokes of light in all directions. Dreadlocks covered his scalp. He wore a leather loincloth while others wore rags. His solemnly flat expression and self-assurance reminded her of Dr. Doom: the certainty that he was never wrong while others mostly were. "Like I asked: what do you have to offer us?"

"I'm a biologist. I could be useful." It astonished her to hear herself say this, but she sensed she must. If Aunt Laney was truly dead, she would need safe harbor. A taint of smoke and sickly sweetness like rotting fruit hung on the air, suggesting menace, as did the sweltering atmosphere. It was no place to be alone. She thought she heard the thrumming of far-off drums. Surely not distant thunder. It hadn't rained in two years, certainly not in October.

"That's the Crystal People," the leader said. "They believe drums repel evil." His followers shook their heads; he remained poker-faced. He held some inexplicable sway over them as all prophets do over their disciples and, like Dr. Doom, brooked no disagreement. An existential absolutist in a world where most harbor doubts. A man who had no use for the niceties of social interaction and did not participate in give and take. It was intimidating. Humans are like other animals that way, she thought. Someone declares, "I am lion king"—always male, always humorless—and few dare contest it.

ONCE SHE'D BECOME A MEMBER of their neo-indigenous tribe, Minah's doubts evaporated. "The Messenger," as they called him, was inscrutable, but she soon came to trust his judgment unconditionally. He knew precisely what needed doing. Such a contrast to Dr. Doom and others of his kind who carped about climate apocalypse but offered no solutions. Such a comfort to find a person who did not merely perceive disaster but had remedies for it as well. Simple and obvious remedies. The only way to save ourselves and the planet, he taught them, is through deprivation. "Fools call it 'self-sacrifice,' I call it 'liberation.' From hunger, want and comfort." They wore nothing but loincloths in the dead of winter, worked half-naked under the scorching summer sun, raised meager garden plots and ate little, slept together in a huge sweat lodge, its dirt floor covered with mattresses salvaged from abandoned houses. The Messenger put her to work finding a remedy for the bed bugs and lice that were a communal plague. Every common cold became a communal infection. She urged the ill to wear masks. He forbade it. Illness, he said, was nature's remedy for overpopulation. Childbearing was taboo. "Our job is to help the human race die off. It's a sin against nature to have children." Drugs of all kinds were forbidden, even analgesics. If pain woke you up at night, it was considered a blessing. Humans should suffer along with the pained earth.

They held group masturbation sessions, stroking their genitals in a cozy circle, leering at each other but not touching. It was the group's single concession to human desire. Touch was forbidden, since it might lead to intimacy and that to childbirth. Moreover, intimacy was a bourgeois sin a dying planet could no longer afford. "Group sex" brought them closer and mated them all to The Messenger.

Secretly, she had begun to fall in love with him, though love was forbidden. How could she not? He was more self-certain than Dr. Doom or anyone else she had ever known. Messianic, really. Tall, erect, his face acorn brown. Seemingly without ethnicity or gender. He was everyone. Androgynous. At times, he/she appeared to have a penis, at others not. Making love to him/her/them, she decided, would be like fucking a star. She could not even look into his face. It was like looking at the naked sun.

One night they raided the Crystal People's enclave and burned their marijuana crop without resistance. No one wanted to mess with them. They were fearless. Pain and death didn't worry them. "The planet is already dead," The Messenger said, "and we along with it." Dr. Doom had said something similar years ago. But what had once frightened her was comforting now. "There are others we must deal with," he told them, "liars and deniers and false prophets."

This brought to mind one of Dr. Doom's lectures. "There will be four kinds of survivors," he said. "The wealthy who are buying up land in Iceland and building fortified compounds out of reach of marauders and social collapse. Gangster sociopaths who prey on the weak, whom I call 'Scalpers.' Thirdly, 'Single Walkers:' individuals who rely on their wits, ingenuity and stealth to survive. Finally, True Believers: Jesus freaks and other faith terrorists, 'avenging angels,' left wing communards, right wing neo-Nazis, all kinds of assorted nutjobs who believe they alone will survive. Some of you will be attracted to such cults because they will offer simple solutions." Saying this, he looked tellingly at Minah. Nonsense, she had thought back then; I'm no joiner.

ON HER FOURTH TRY, LANEY FOUND the O'Ryan's bunker with the help of hell hounds, as she called them, that dug down to the concrete roof, attracted by the smell of food inside. She finished digging dirt away from the trapdoor, and opened it with trepidation, fearing the O'Ryan's moldering corpses might be trapped inside. They weren't. But many pounds of dried corn, beans, rice, canned meats and fruit were stacked on metal shelves, untouched by mold or rodents. She was giggling in delight when she heard voices overhead. At first, she froze in terror. Then hurried up the ladder, fearing whoever it was might close the door on her, and was astonished to see perhaps a dozen people approaching in nothing but flimsy loincloths.

"Hi, Aunt Laney," a middle-aged woman called, her round face vaguely familiar, looking something like her brother, Jerry. "I'm very happy to see you. I wasn't sure you were still alive."

"Minah?" she cried. "My god! It's been twenty-five years. What are you doing here? Half-naked to boot? It must be forty degrees."

"Suffering builds character," a young woman insisted. "It prepares us for what's coming."

"And what's that?"

The girl made no reply, but a hulk of a man with a coarse, weather-worn face, hair in tight ringlets and a braided blond beard falling to his navel said, "*That* is as bad as anything humans have ever faced, likely worse. We must steel ourselves."

Laney gestured at the charred desolation around them. "Here's suffering for you: four hundred residents burned and so did thousands of trees. Suffering is overrated. Who are these people, Minah?" she asked the niece she hadn't seen since she was a girl.

"'Survivors.' This is The Messenger." Minah gestured at the man with the braided beard decorated with bright beads. He didn't quite smile but displayed a mouthful of widely-spaced teeth. Like a goat's, she thought. His yellow irises appeared to pulse in their sockets. He put her on guard, even more so than the boy Moss who had locked her in her bunker months ago. "What do you people want? There's nothing left up here but ash and burned houses."

"With food stashes beneath. Right, grandma?" The Messenger grinned menacingly; his followers giggled.

"I'm nobody's grandma," she snapped.

The brazen, half-naked girl said, "Even if we eat just only enough to stay alive, we still have to eat. The Messenger was instructed to come up here."

"Instructed by whom? To take what isn't yours to take?"

"Not yours to take either," her niece snapped. "That's your house—" she pointed "—this isn't. I remember the granite boulder above it."

"The only house still standing on the mountain," a tall man said accusatorially.

"The O'Ryans would want me to have their supplies, as I would want them to have mine. We were friends."

"Ownership no longer applies," The Messenger said. "Didn't the fire teach you people nothing? What's yours is ours; what's ours is anybody's." His acolytes nodded at what Laney imagined was a slogan to them. He waved two of them down into the bunker. Cults that had sprung up since the end of normal times spooked Laney given their presumption of entitlement, communal privilege, and secret knowledge. Faith freaks, Crystal People, Avengers, Truth Talkers, Survivalists. Dangerous people.

"It must be nice to have all the answers," Laney said. "I don't. At least I admit it."

Her niece laughed. "She was sarcastic like that when I was a girl."

Laney asked her, "Do you really think this man cares about you? Do you think any of them do? They are loyal to a hollow fantasy, not to other people. I know; I grew up with that."

They surrounded her, their irises appearing to pulsate to the same hypnotic rhythm. With a nod of the head The Messenger could have them on her. "I was going to leave you a token for leading us to this," he said. "Your greed has changed my mind. She who lives by sacrifice earns charity; she who doesn't earns nothing." Several of them drummed their bare chests in assent.

She remembered that she had left the hatch to her own bunker wide open. They would strip it bare and likely commandeer her house and leave her nothing. A desperate, inchoate plan came to her, which, hopefully, would fill out in its undertaking.

"Come up to the house with me, Minah. I have pictures of you and your sister Cassidy you will want to see." Telling the Messenger, "Minah's younger sister was lost to her years ago, likely taken by sex slavers. Minah was devastated."

"Minah doesn't need to be reminded of her lost sister," he said. "What's done is done. We're all lost now, every one of us." More chest-thumping agreement.

"You can have the O'Ryan's stash," Laney persisted. "It's all yours."

Minah seemed torn between The Messenger and a desire to see her beloved sister's face again. Laney gripped her elbow and started off. He ordered the adolescent girl to go with them.

While the two of them looked at family pictures on the corkboard, Laney slipped into the bedroom to retrieve her pistol from the night table. Returning to the room, she pointed it stiff-armed at them. "Not a peep! I will shoot." Fully believing she was capable of it. "Tie the dish towel over the girl's mouth, Minah, and her arms behind her back with that electric cord. I don't trust her; she's brainwashed. I'm not sure about you yet. At least we're family."

She marched them behind the house to her underground bunker, out of sight of The Messenger's crew, Minah's hands raised stiffly in the air. It didn't hurt that she thought her aunt a touch crazy. Laney ordered them down into the bunker, untying the girl's hands when she was on the top step of the ladder, closing the hatch behind them and covering it with ashes. Then she marched over the cinders with a metallic rustling toward the O'Ryan place, the pistol hidden behind her back. The Messenger turned toward her as she approached, his eyebrows arching when she brought the gun out. "What have you done with my girls?"

"They are in a safe place. I may release them when you're gone." She surmised that he wouldn't risk much to keep a couple of chicks in his flock. There were plenty of desperate people to recruit. Likely he wouldn't return; there were other bunkers to sack. But you couldn't be sure of anything anymore. She allowed them to retreat with a pillowcase full of goods, hands raised stiffly over their heads until they were out of sight.

"I want you off my mountain," she barked at the girl after calling her and Minah up from the bunker, their faces white as bleached sheets. They had feared that she would leave them down in that cold, dark hole. "I'd like you to stay here with me, Minah. You are family and seemingly need a home."

Her niece appeared to assess this: stay or return to The Messenger? She nodded. "You were Cassidy's favorite," she said. "We loved visiting you on the mountain." Her eyes surveyed the devastation around them: a graveyard of charred stumps, thick trails of ash where trees had fallen, the white-washed gray sky stretching out over the valley, barely distinguishable from the ground beneath it. She grimaced as if trying to comprehend it. "I could help you plant trees," she decided.

Laney nodded. "I could use your help. You...Git!" She jabbed the gun at the girl, who slipped and slid over the ash as she fled down the slope, looking like a marionette with a broken guide string.

DREAM TIME

I must assume the headlights I catch glimpses of in the rearview mirror as I wend through the Coast Range somewhere near Covelo belong to Mirabella Estragado's antique Isuzu. No one else is crazy enough to be on the road. She has followed me from Los Angeles. I can't imagine how she navigates sharp curves and precipitous downgrades in her petrol-powered SUV with its ponderous load. Where does she find fuel? The last gas stations closed fifteen years ago. But I suppose if you can carry all of humanity inside your car you don't need fuel. It's powered by hope. Or despair.

I'm close to empty. The warning light flashes on the dashboard and the fuel gauge has the shivers. No hydro-fuel stations out here. I would be wise to take a logging road into the woods and ditch the car before I run out, conceal my rig under foliage so the Liberty Patrol won't spot it from the air while trolling in search of climate refugees. We are far from the southern border, but their paranoia knows no bounds. Trouble is, I would have to trek on foot fifty miles, back and forth from Wilderness Road, to retrieve supplies one backpack full at a time. No way I can carry all the supplies stashed under the backseat and false trunk of my car in a single load: dried corn, beans, lentils, and root crops, enough to tide me over for months, along with provisions already stowed in my refuge. The great twentieth-century writer Gabriel Garcia Marquez told us "Life is a constant opportunity for survival." It has become the anthem of our time. Along with Granny K's advice: "Don't despair, prepare."

We are traveling through territory prone to wildfires. Some miles back, we passed through a forest of charcoal snags glistening in the moonlight. A devious beauty, strange and alien. We had to creep around deadfalls blocking the road. Now, instinctively, I cut the lights and stop my car before rounding a bend in the road, get out and walk ahead. *Cultivate instinct*, another anthem. A bonfire burns mid-road several hundred yards below, doubtless a roadblock manned by armed local militia to keep intruders out of their territory. Dark figures move about with torches like watchmen from an earlier time. I run back and stand mid-road, waving my arms at Mirabella to cut her lights and engine, hurry to her window and whisper, "*¡Alto! Peligro*," pointing ahead. Her engine sounds like a freight train in the quiet forest. She kills it. "Roadblock," I say. Her English may not be good enough to understand what I'm saying, and my Spanish isn't good enough to convey it. I sense those billions of human souls packed into her car listening intently. How does she communicate with them? They speak hundreds of different tongues. Maybe all human souls speak the same language in the end. Mirabella is one of the few living people who can communicate with them. Although some contend that none of us are truly alive anymore. We hover somewhere between life and death, suspended in a dream.

It occurs to me that few others in history have addressed such a big audience. Although Mirabella likely ranted non-stop about *El Diablo* all the way up here, begging them to pray to *El Señor* with her. I doubt they did; we are well past prayer now.

Why follow me? Do they think I will find us a safe haven when I'm running out of fuel and don't know how I will reach my destination or what I will find when I get there? I can't trust my own judgment. I suffer blackouts. Sometimes I sit in the fortified backyard of my L.A. compound talking to former occupants, ghosts from a kinder time. Perhaps they have chosen my leadership because I knew it was time to abandon L.A. Because I'm foolish enough to travel through perilous territory. Because I trust that Fate will give us a break when we need it most.

I park my hydro-van in the woods and move stealthily through the forest along the road, together with a crew of Mirabella's passengers—can't say how many since I can't see them. Doubtless, there are fierce warriors from earlier times among them: Roman legionaries, Genghis Kahn's butchers, Viking Berserkers. Still, we are no match for the crew blocking the road ahead even in our millions. Not in all of human history have there been warriors as fierce as survivors of our ongoing horror. Existential warriors. A new kind of human, annealed in the heat of annihilation. We hide silently in thick foliage, watching. Maybe ten of them armed to the teeth, casting menacing shadows, faces stained blood red in firelight. The souls around me whisper in a faltering susurrus of trepidation. I make out FDR's voice telling us there's nothing to fear but fear itself. Maybe that was true once, but no longer. No way we can make our way past. Even if we slink through the woods as quiet as field mice, their keen senses will pick us up. We return to my car. I whisper, "We don't dare move ahead down Highway 162 or wherever we are with those Scalpers blocking the way, and don't dare return to L.A. This logging road must lead somewhere, likely to an abandoned survivalist camp. You should be safe there. I will try to reach my place in Branscomb. Not room for all of us there I'm afraid."

Suddenly, Mirabella's car streaks down the road past us, honking and crashing through barricades, throwing Scalpers and hot embers into the woods. Flames instantly engulf tinder-dry brush and race up trees that have known no rain for years. Orange needles that are dead from bark beetle infestation explode; fire creeps along dead limbs sticking skeletally out all sides. I leap into my car and race down the dirt track deeper into the trees, plowing through brush. Mirabella's souls will survive the fire. Many of them have already been cremated. I run out of fuel just as the road ends. It seems an omen. I cram all I can carry into my backpack: dried legumes, seeds from my garden, my father's old deer rifle, warm clothes. Canned goods are too heavy to tote. Little hope of returning for them. My car will be incinerated. The air is already thick with acrid smoke; fire races through tree crowns a few hundred yards away. I feel its heat against my cheeks.

The animal path leading down a steep slope will hopefully take me below the fire. An opportunity for survival since fire prefers to run uphill. Along with the smell of pine needles, the air is full of nostalgia. Memories of kinder days. The temperature, in the mid-eighties before the fire started (would have been in the low forties this time of year in normal times), must be over a hundred now. My damp shirt clings to my skin. I half-run, half-slide downhill, carried along by the weight of my load.

BEFORE I LEFT, COYOTES AND MOUNTAIN LIONS roamed the streets of Los Angeles, keeping the stray dog population down, a blessing since wild dogs formed packs that attacked anything, man or beast, as dangerous to us when we ventured out of our compounds as Scalpers were. Water trickled from spigots and wasn't safe to drink; LA Power and Water was on an emergency footing. Not enough water to keep my vegetable garden alive. I bathed out of a bucket and shit in a hole in the backyard. Trees lining boulevards were dying even in Beverly Hills, lawns gone brown. Beyond drought, there was the heat, kidnappings, break-ins, criminal cartels and hungry climate refugees to worry about. I slept with the rifle in bed beside me.

By my early twenties, years ago, I knew we were in peril. "You see disaster everywhere you look," my ex-wife Denise scolded me. "Well, isn't it?" I replied. Locked away in my compound toward the end, I sometimes wondered if I was going mad. I sat in Granny K's backyard fortress looking up at stars illuminating the dark sky in a city devoid of light pollution on those many nights the power was out. A display as splendid as it must have been two hundred years ago. We were going backwards. Former occupants of the house sat beside me: World War Two Vet Delgado, dead eighty years now, strange William who had rented a room from Granny K and died of lung cancer long ago. It didn't seem odd to me that phantoms walked among us. After all, nature has become a phantom. "Strange, isn't it," I said, "that we are returning to the past rather than moving forward to the future?" William laughed derisively. "What future?" Delgado waved a hand at him. "In my day, we believed in the future, but today fear and pessimism has screwed people up." William howled laughter. "Hey, man, everything we've ever done has screwed us up, including your stinking war. Nature has had enough of us."

If mine was madness, it was collective madness at a time when sanity no longer made sense. We all longed for saner times. Nostalgia had become an obsession. Old folks fantasized about cool spring nights. The young walked around in a daze before it was too dangerous to be outside, staring down at blank cell phone screens, dark since microwave transmissions went down years ago.

The Liberty Network and Truth Seekers, who had cornered what remained of the Internet, reported horrors. The air in Mumbai, home to thirty-two million people, had become too toxic to breathe. Millions died of respiratory failure, and COVID SARSX-2 preyed on weakened survivors. The atmosphere in most urban zones was a soup of mordant chemicals similar to Jupiter's atmosphere, hostile to all forms of life. Intense heat, interacting with petrochemicals used in the production of neo-plastics, methane gas released from melting permafrost in Greenland, and CO2 exhaled from the lungs of machines and humans in overcrowded cities, spawned new forms of pneumonia unresponsive to antibiotics. China's megalopolises were sweltering dead zones. Its madcap race to prosperity had sealed its doom. Not enough people survived to bury the dead, and bodies rotted in the street, hosting new strains of bacteria that fed on festering flesh. Gruesome horrors. London, Pakistan and Bangladesh suffered regular flooding. Heat and dust from North Africa blanketed Southern Europe. Rome and Athens often reached 120 degrees Fahrenheit, close to lethal for humans, and dust pollution darkened the sky. This at a mere 2.3 degrees of warming. It's expected to hit four by century's end.

Few trustworthy news outlets remained to confirm these horrors. But we knew that the "Ozymandias Zone," as we called it, encompassing the Southwestern U.S., faced perpetual drought far beyond the Dustbowl of the 1930s. Phoenix and Vegas were deserted. Sand mounded up in the abandoned lobbies of casinos. Cities in the American South and East endured Noahic flooding from hurricanes, atmospheric rivers and sea level rise. New Orleans and Miami Beach were half submerged, while the Mississippi River had become a mere trickle. New York was holding out, given its elaborate system of sea walls and locks rapidly constructed during the Thirties. But for how long? Its residents were hungry, as people most everywhere were. Civilization was a boxer on the ropes taking a nonstop pummeling. William was right: after thousands of years of subjugation, nature was fighting back.

Granny K knew what was coming long before most and hoarded food and water through the Twenties, stashed on shelves in her fortified basement: cans of corn, beets, split pea soup, tuna, sacks of flour and dry goods, three-hundred gallons of bottled water. Before supply chain issues made hoarding impossible. "When I was a girl, people built bomb shelters and stocked them with supplies," she told me. "That was paranoia. What we face now is a dead certainty. We're running out of water and food and killing each other for what remains."

By 2060, I realized I would need to escape L.A. soon and went in search of a refuge in the outbacks of Mendocino County in Northern California, hoarding hydro-fuel rations to get there. I found Branscomb, an old logging town that had been just a wide spot in the road in its heyday: a few houses, a general store and post office, and a sprawling sawmill with huge stacks of redwood logs awaiting the saws.

Deserted now; the sawmill's buildings rusting, grounds littered with scraps of wood, and cranes slumping toward the ground. West of town, Wilderness Road meandered into the woods along a branch of the nearly dry Eel River. The few houses along it were abandoned, the road blocked in places by fallen trees, suggesting that no one occupied these woods. But you couldn't be sure. I found an overgrown track leading up into the timber, clearly unused. A tumbledown cabin sat in a clearing a quarter mile up. Its owner had likely died long ago, although it wouldn't have mattered since ownership had little standing anymore. You owned what you could take and hold onto, as it was for millennia before the false promise of civilization and myth of private ownership. Remarkably, there was an old well. Avoiding the cabin and its resident ghosts, I built a crude shelter in a huge burned-out redwood stump nearby. Its fire-hardened walls glistened like obsidian. I camouflaged the shake roof with tree boughs, so that from afar my shelter blended into the forest. Every few months, I transported canned goods Granny K had stashed in the basement before she died, plus dried beans and corn I'd grown in my backyard garden, and other essentials to my refuge, preparing for the day I would flee the city. All stowed in a larder dug into the side of a hill. My life would be lonely on Wilderness Road, but not as lonely as it was living among people who feared each other.

After UCLA closed its doors and the city and state governments began to collapse, I knew it was time to leave. All went down fast. The National Guard stopped distributing government commodities. People were hungry and desperate. I heard gunshots outside my barricaded windows. No ambulances remained to take victims to St. Johns Providence, the single hospital still open, although its doctors had mostly fled. If you wanted to design a city ideally suited to anarchy, you couldn't do better than Los Angeles. I loaded my car and fled to Branscomb, knowing I might not have enough fuel to reach it.

AFTER ESCAPING THE FIRE, I TREK all night through the Coast Range, following logging roads west toward the big trees. Redwoods are faring better than most other trees given their defenses against wildfire—thick bark and high overstory. The gibbous moon in a clear sky provides enough light for me to find my way. Moreover, my night vision kicks in. It's as if I'm walking through earlier days when homo sapiens traversed mountain paths without artificial light to guide them. Quite literally, I have returned to the past.

I sense other beings in the woods. Perhaps Native Americans stalking me. Or Bigfoot. If I were to bet on who will survive the climate holocaust, I would choose the Sasquatch, who have survived unseen among us for thousands of years. Or indigenous peoples, who know how to live with Nature and find opportunities for survival no matter how harsh the conditions, who see themselves as nature's children rather than its masters. I would bet on them.

Even in that dim light, I make out footprints in the dust—bare feet and hooves. It worries me that stirrings in the brush could be domestic pigs gone feral, as dangerous as wild boars. I keep my rifle at the ready, walking dead center of a narrow track that clings to the mountainside, hoping to avoid a plunge into a densely wooded canyon below. Haze from deep canyons dances around me in ghostly wisps. The ravines are like troughs in the sea: ancient, untracked, unreachable. No telling how tall the redwoods are down there or if streams still flow, providing water for the huge ape-men who shuffle through the big trees feasting on berries. Such a creature could remain hidden in this wilderness for centuries. The coast range has been compared to a human brain, given its many folds and convolutions, its wonders.

Suddenly, with not so much as a breath of wind to announce its arrival, a storm hits. The sky closes, blocking the moon; it's dark as a tomb. Heavy rain pounds my head and shoulders as if I am under a waterfall. An unnerving roar. I am soaked through before I can dig my rain slicker out of the backpack. Wind picks up off the ocean and the temperature drops forty degrees. My teeth chatter, water drips off my chin, puddles underfoot soak through my shoes. I can't find my flashlight. I dare not move blindly ahead through the murk, dare not stay put either. I make my way toward a thicket I saw before the rain started, hoping to find shelter, hands extended before me to ward off branches. Suddenly the ground falls away and I step into thin air in free fall.

It seems like I fall for half a minute, long enough to wonder how my life could end so pointlessly. But likely, it's only a second before I land feet first on a narrow ledge, unhurt but teetering over the abyss, my feet mired in mud. A reprieve beyond any I have ever known. I reach out and bury my hands in moist clay. I might just remain here, clinging to my impossible perch on a steep mountainside, but rain lashes down, liquefying mud. I've heard of entire hillsides slumping away in mud avalanches. Fearing I will lose my footing, perched precariously as I am, the backpack adding to gravity's remorseless pull, I claw uphill with fingers, elbows, feet, like some impossible centipede, inching my way up through the muck.

I can't say how long I climb. Moving in slow time, the nontime you experience when a disturbing dream wakes you into insomnia, and you have no idea how long you lie in a stupor, your mind racing through a confusion of images from moments in your life melded together in a numinous haze wherein everything happens at once and you are neither quite conscious nor unconscious. Somewhere between. In dream time. Something gratifying in it, even comforting at this perilous moment. A state mostly unknown to modern man and nearly impossible for us to fathom in our frantic world, our whirlwind of what we take to be forward momentum.

Then I slither up over the verge onto the road and crawl across it on hands and knees into a scratchy Manzanita thicket, its slick, peeling bark unmistakable to the touch. I sit laughing and crying in turn, howling like a dog. I'm covered head to toe in clay-thick muck: hair, face, clothes, backpack...in my ears, between my toes. I spit it out of my mouth, lift my face to the sky and let the rain wash it clean, lather hair with my fingers. Mud runs down into my shirt. I stand up in a clearing midpoint of that small thicket, strip bare and shower in the downpour, shivering cold but exhilarated. I wash my clothes with rainwater and hang them from branches, then put on my rain slicker to shield myself from wind that lashes branches overhead and whistles through treetops. Hypothermia is a danger. I do calisthenics to get my blood flowing and run furiously in place.

Then, as suddenly as they came, the rain and wind stop, the sky clears, the moon is clean and new, its light half-blinding after the darkness. Feeling reborn, I don my wet clothes and start off, the first hint of dawn behind me.

I avoid Dos Rios, which is barricaded and defended by wary residents who fear strangers like we all do. I hide in the brush overlooking Highway 101, not far from the former town of Laytonville, watching for an opportunity to cross.

No cars, other than the burned carcass of a pickup at the side of the road. It is fellow trekkers who worry me, climate vagrants, desperate folks. Individually, they are dangerous. In groups, deadly. Seeing no one, I dash across the highway like a deer and crash into brush on the far side.

I BUILD SMALL CAMPFIRES IN THE TINY meadow behind the cabin near Wilderness Road, even though I'm wary about fire and know it can be seen flickering through the trees. But surely I am alone out here in my kingdom of one. Days are busy with chores: cutting firewood with a bow saw, collecting apples from abandoned orchards and acorns that I leach tannic acid out of and boil into a mush that the native Pomos called "wewish"—insipid but carbohydrate rich. I plant a winter garden—greens and root crops that I irrigate by hand, lugging water in a bucket from the well—and set snares for rabbits and squirrels. I build an oven, using clay hauled up from the river bank a quarter mile away. No end of things to do when you are struggling to survive. But nights are long, lonely, and boring. I sit meditating on the flickering campfire, my mind stumbling through memories of Denise and my girls, whom I haven't seen in years, how they loved to ride on my back and the impromptu skits Harmony enacted, my teaching and book tours and brief love affairs with students. I miss human touch, but have for years now. I recall my childhood back in normal times: summer camp and backyard football with the neighborhood boys, first dates and first sex, ski trips to Big Bear—before snow stopped falling for good. I've never been into social media, but long for it now—any human contact. Isolated as I am, I could be in outer space.

One night I see eyes glowing in the firelight near the cabin. Too close to the ground to be human. A lynx or raccoon or coyote? A feral hog? I've seen signs of bear. The eyes know I've seen them; we watch each other. The rifle leans against a tree thirty feet away. If the creature charges, I won't have time to reach it. I sit perfectly still, breathing slowly.

It creeps cautiously forward into the firelight: a dog that looks like a wolf, a domesticated wolf perhaps. I am about to sprint for the gun, knowing others could be hidden in the trees, when it trots forward out of the shadows, whining and wagging its tail, drops to its haunches before me in a display of submission, cocking its head up.

"Well hello there, fellow. Where did you come from?" I scratch between his ears and under his chin. He nuzzles my knees in instant friendship. No collar, but clearly domesticated. Doubtless left behind by a fleeing resident. Morbidly thin. His eyes hungry, begging. I am likely the first human it has seen in months. "I suppose you'd like something to eat?" I face an important decision: if I invite the dog to join me, there will be another mouth to feed, but I will gain a loyal friend and ally at a time when I desperately need one. I lower a haunch of smoked venison, hung out of reach of predators from a rope thrown over a tree branch, a bit nervous that the dog will attack me and take it all. But he lies watching, chin on paws. The starving fellow downs chunks of meat I slice off in a few bites, then digs into a bowl of beans left over from my dinner, licking the bowl clean.

"You're welcome to sleep here with me." For days it has been too hot to sleep inside, although well into November. I feel comfortable having him here. It's the first time in weeks I've slept without remaining on high alert.

I've never made a friend so quickly in my life. "I'm going to name you 'Pal,'" I tell him next morning, "because I need one." He accompanies me that afternoon when I check trap lines, becoming agitated smelling a snare that holds remnants of animal fur. Some creature has made off with my catch. Pal sniffs madly about, dodging into the trees. Farther on, he goes on high alert, hackles up, growling and advancing on a wild huckleberry thicket in a crouch. "What is it?" I ask. "Who's there?" No answer, but I sense a presence as Pal does. We stomp about in the brush but find no trace of anything.

The next day I spot what is surely a human figure slinking through the trees. A fellow hermit? Urban refugee? A sprite? Seemingly as nervous about me as I am about it. Pal doesn't give chase but stands whining beside me.

THERE ARE FOOTPRINTS AROUND the well the next morning, human and barefoot. Surely left overnight, but Pal didn't bark. This mystifies me; he is always so alert. He growls at pileated woodpeckers flying overhead. Someone is using my well, possibly the person I saw in the woods or whoever looted abandoned houses on Wilderness Road. There isn't enough water in the well to share. Sometimes the bucket scrapes against the rocky bottom when I lower it. I sit beside the well that night along with Pal, rifle across my knees, repeatedly dozing off and starting awake. At first light, I wake up exhausted. It's already hot, maybe ninety degrees, and I am soaked with sweat. Pal looks up at me rebukingly, as if to ask, *Why are you doing this to me?* Because, of course, dogs think we control the weather. In that way they are a lot like many of us, believing some higher power is in control of our lives. "Look, Pal, it's not my fault. . . . Holy shit!" Footprints circle the chair I'm sitting on. Scuff marks, as if the creature had shuffled its feet trying to get a closer look at me. "What the hell! Why didn't you bark?" Pal sniffs the prints, but seems to smell nothing. "Spirits, do you think, boy? Souls from Mirabella's car that followed me here? But they wouldn't leave physical traces; they're incorporeal."

We remain on high alert all day, checking the undergrowth when we hear something stir, although we can barely move in the stupefying heat. The overheated brain slows to a crawl. I can't concentrate, can't remember what is troubling me, am afraid my blackouts will return. I've had none here under the calming presence of the big trees, whose roots tangle in a matrix underfoot, sending up soothing vibes that assure me I am welcome here. No need for mind numbing out here far from the toxic detritus of civilization.

Even trees seem stressed by the heat; their exhausted branches sag groundward. The few remaining old-growth redwoods have lost their shadows under the blazing sun. I feel their pain. It's all I can do to haul buckets of water to my garden, where I find the spinach depleted, lettuce leaves scattered about, sweet potatoes pulled out of the ground. Deer? Wild Pigs? Raccoons? How could they penetrate the thickets of Manzanita fencing in my plots? Thieving humans? "Look, you bastards," I shout into the woods, "grow your own fucking garden. This one is mine."

As if in answer, the wind picks up and is soon thrashing crowns of the big trees, whipping huge branches side to side—hot and dry, full of grit that pocks my face. A Santa Ana way up here? Impossible. Pal crawls under a ceanothus bush. He will be covered with ticks when he emerges. Then, as if I have invited it, the wind turns icy cold, and I am quickly chilled through. The rain will come, I know, as it did on the mountain. I've grown close enough to nature to predict its doings. It does, as if blasted from a fire hose: hot rain. I've never experienced anything like it, neither have the trees. I sense their anxiety. Pal follows me to the shelter, which holds up for maybe five minutes before wind tears off the roof and warm rainwater rises in the bowl formed by shelter walls. A mini-tornado whips my possessions upward in a vortex. I seize Pal's hind legs just as he begins twirling upward. Somehow I make it to the cabin, pulling him behind me like a kite. Remarkable what strength adrenaline provides. We require it for flight and fight. Maybe nature does too. Maybe that's what it is in the end—storms, heat, hurricanes, rising sea waters—nature empowered by its own mighty adrenaline in the face of human assault, enhanced by the energy a warming planet provides it.

One disaster follows another in rapid succession. It snows a foot one day in a place where it never snows. The trees seem bewildered. I can almost see them shrugging their shoulders, shaking this cold white stuff off their branches. It's so hot the next day that snow melts by ten A.M. Then more rain, accompanied by a mudslide that buries the entrance to my larder cave. I work furiously to dig away mud before it hardens to concrete under the merciless sun. A seam opens up near the river and the smell of tar wafts up to me. It forms a pool like the La Brea tar pits, burbling hot, stinking like a sulfuric hell hole. Animals become trapped in the gooey stuff: a fawn, an over-curious raccoon, a wild pig. The smell of barbecued pork fills the air. Pal stands at the brink and barks. I seize his collar and pull him away. Then try to lasso one of the pig's legs with a rope I've fashioned of twisted clothes, hoping to pull it out and smoke the meat.

That night, when rain thunders down on the cabin's roof and I fear it will collapse, I have an epiphany. I realize that all of these extreme events are happening at once. All of time. It is both today, the Anthropocene, and the end of the Pleistocene at once, when oil burbled to the surface and Mammoths became mired in it. Both raining with an aching chill that gets into your bones and parching dry. These huge trees are both bursting with life—storing carbon and releasing oxygen into the air—and lying dead and rotten on the forest floor, hosting beetles and fungi and releasing carbon back into the atmosphere. I, too, am both robust and dying. Flesh withers on my arms. Pal's skeleton lies on the cabin floor at my feet. Despite this, and possibly even because of it, I experience a peace I have never known before and realize that I am so inextricably bound with nature that there is no separating us. I am no more alone than the trees or bracken fern on the forest floor or the blue jay that wakes me up with its raucous call. We are all part of the whole. The death of a single microbe amounts to no less than my own death, the weight of the entire universe is no greater than my own tiny mass, because we are one and the same. No separating past and present, past and future. What is happening now has happened before and will happen again. Wanton destruction, then rebirth, the world blooming again. Both at once. We are in dream time. Existentially, there is nothing to fear. Yes, my paltry life will end in its present form, but aren't all those souls in Mirabella's car proof that it will continue in some mysterious way beyond anything we can comprehend?

Then suddenly Pal is clothed in flesh and fur again, up barking and scratching at the door. I get up and throw it open unhesitatingly. Nothing to fear. Now that I am inextricably bonded with nature in a way I never imagined possible, it makes no difference whether it is an infuriated brown bear or starving feral hog or the wind at my door. Or what it turns out to be: nothing. Nothing I can see, anyway, but I sense its presence. Some wandering native boy, perhaps, who lost his way and didn't realize he was dead, who came across this strange dwelling in the woods and asked to enter to get out of the rain. "Come in, come in," I throw the door open wide. "Come sit by the fire and warm yourself." Pal leaps forward to smell him. Bewildered, likely, that this visitor has no form but carries with it the smell of both the living and the dead. He sneezes repeatedly, then wags his tail and backs away to let the stranger in.

"Do come in and tell us your story," I say. "But could you please close the door behind you?"

It closes with a soft thump. At that instant, the rain stops falling.

ACKNOWLEDGMENTS

An excerpt from "The Three Devils" appeared in *The Corona Chronicles* anthology from *Cutthroat: A Journal of the Arts* (November, 2021): pp 121-146.

An excerpt from "How Trouble Begins" appeared in the anthology *Through The Ash, New Leaves* published by *Cutthroat: A Journal of the Arts* and The Black Earth Institute (Spring, 2022 #27, Vol. 1): pp 243-8.

"Dr. Doom and the Messenger" appeared in *Emerald City Magazine* in Summer 2024.

* * *

Grateful thanks to all those members of the Cornerstone team who have helped make this book a reality—from editing to cover design to promotion and more—and to the University of Wisconsin–Stevens Point. Special thanks to Dr. Ross K. Tangedal, Director and Publisher, Grace Dahl, Senior Editor, and proofreader Cora C. Bender for their help and enthusiasm. It has been a pleasure working with them.

All writers need support for their work. I am grateful to the many fellow writers, editors, publishers and friends who have championed my work over the years. First among them my wife Lucinda Luvaas, always my first and most valued reader. I also owe special thanks to Mary Tondorf-Dick, Managing Editor at Little, Brown, who selected my first novel, *The Seductions of Natalie Bach*, off the slush pile—one of just three un-agented books LB published in twenty years. Thanks as well to my Jefferson Park neighborhood in Los Angeles that partly inspired several stories in *The Three Devils*. For my wife (a painter and filmmaker) and I, our place is both a home and year-round art colony, including her studio in the backyard that we built with our own hands. Our beloved akita Mimi is pet-in-residence at the colony.

William Luvaas has published four novels, *The Seductions of Natalie Bach* (1986), *Going Under* (1994), *Beneath The Coyote Hills* (2016), and *Welcome To Saint Angel* (2018), plus two story collections: *A Working Man's Apocrypha* (2007) and *Ashes Rain Down* (2013), which was *The Huffington Post*'s 2013 Book of the Year. He lives in Los Angeles with his wife, Lucinda.

www.ingramcontent.com/pod-product-compliance
Lightning Source LLC
Chambersburg PA
CBHW030952170125
20531CB00041B/536

* 9 7 8 1 9 6 0 3 2 9 6 2 2 *